Roses are Red, Violet is Dead

An Abby Spector Ghost Mystery

MORGAN SPELLMAN

MEADOW CAT

Published by Meadow Cat Press
An imprint of Meadow Cat, LLC

ISBN (print): 979-8-9885795-2-6
ISBN (ebook): 979-8-9885795-3-3

For permissions, inquiries, or questions, please contact:
meadowcatpress@gmail.com

First Edition: February 2024

Cover design by Holly Dunn Design

1 2 3 4 5 6 7 8 9 10

www.MorganSpellman.com

*For anyone looking for a
heartwarming ghost mystery*

Abby Spector Ghost Mystery Series

AN ABBY SPECTOR GHOST MYSTERY

Roses are Red, Violet is Dead

MORGAN SPELLMAN

Prologue

Abby felt like a thief as she watched a dark van back out of the driveway.

But she wasn't after their property. She was after one thing—the ghost that may or may not be haunting their house.

After taking a hearty sip of her red velvet latte, she unbuckled her seatbelt, tucked her brass binoculars under her hoodie, and scrambled out of her blue Volkswagen as quietly as possible. The leafless trees offered little shade as the sun blazed across half-frozen sidewalks and freshly trimmed hedges.

Abby hurried past a mailbox marked *103 Blackthorn Lane* and turned down the driveway, where the van had been. She rushed across the side yard, following the stone path she had memorized so many years ago. Eventually, the path gave way to frosted grass that crunched under her sneakers as she moved deeper into the backyard.

Taking a deep breath of cold February air, she raised the binoculars. The yard lost its vibrancy, settling into a muted gray. The deck transformed into a kaleidoscope, revealing the echoes of its many iterations throughout the years—the ghosts of various tables, grills, and chairs competing for space. The scene stirred Abby's memories: recollections of cookouts, whispered secrets, and heartfelt promises spoken in this very yard bubbled to the surface. Abby pushed them aside, turning her attention to the vacant windows.

There were no signs of anyone, living or dead.

Abby switched on the walkie-talkie clipped to her jeans and whispered, "Chelsea?"

She held her breath, waiting. Hoping. Longing. Ever since Abby had learned ghosts were real, and acquired the gear to talk to them, there was only one ghost she yearned to speak with: her first love, Chelsea Summers. It had taken Abby a few weeks to work up the courage to come back here, to Chelsea's former home. And even then, her hands had trembled so hard she could barely grip the binoculars. Her friend Lucas had been with her then. They had walked up to the front door, claiming to have a flat tire, and asked if they could wait inside while someone came for help. Abby had searched the whole house. There had been no sign of Chelsea.

And yet, she couldn't help but feel like she had overlooked something. She hadn't looked hard enough, or maybe Chelsea's ghost had been resting. She could not help but return, week after week, just to make sure.

Lowering the binoculars, she slipped the walkie-talkie from her hip. Raising the springy antique antenna, she whispered slightly louder, "Chelsea? It's me. It's Abby."

The wind picked up, ruffling Abby's short hair against her face.

Her phone rang.

Abby jumped, startled. She dropped the walkie-talkie and binoculars as she fumbled for her phone in the back pocket of her jeans.

She silenced it before checking the caller ID. Her mother. Rolling her eyes, she answered the call and kneeled to gather her equipment. "Hi, Mom, can I call you back? I'm kind of in the middle of something?"

"You're always in the middle of something. But I'll be quick. Your cousin called."

"Which cousin?"

"Sam."

Abby wrinkled her brow in confusion. While she and Sam had spent most of their childhood summers together, she hadn't seen or heard from Sam outside of the occasional Rosh Hashanah dinner. Their friendship had pretty much halted one Purim a few years ago, when Abby had accidentally locked them out of the car and they had waited for hours in a cold Walmart parking lot, wrapped in thin costume cloaks. They had shared a bottle of chocolate wine while Abby had sobbed uncontrollably over Chelsea and Sam vented about a recent ex.

"What does Sam want?"

Her mother sighed. "They heard about your stunt at the Kensingtons' and want to know if you can help with…"

"With what?" Abby prompted. "A wedding?"

Her mother made a faint hissing sound, inhaling sharply through gritted teeth. At last, she said, "A *ghost* problem."

Abby's heart fluttered with excitement. In all her hard work of getting set up as a paranormal investigation agency, Abby had never imagined her first customer would come from her skeptical mother. "And how did Sam hear I'm an expert at ghost hunting?"

In the silence that followed, she imagined her mother pinching the bridge of her nose.

Abby grinned.

"Call them if you want, or don't," Rebecca snapped. "Just *be careful*. I mean it. I don't want you jumping off rooftops."

"That was one time," Abby insisted. "And I didn't jump. It was more of a makeshift zip line."

"I'll text you Sam's number. And remember, even though they're family, you should charge appropriately."

"Mom," Abby whined. It was bad enough when her mother criticized her job choices; she hated that she was now trying to control how she ran her business.

"Don't give more than a fifteen percent discount. And maybe add a liability clause."

"Mom!"

"I'm not kidding, Abby. If you go around burning benches or knocking holes in things, you could be hit with a huge property damage—"

"I'm hanging up now." Abby lowered the phone from her ear. "Thanks for calling."

She ended the call and picked up her fallen equipment, turning up the volume of the walkie-talkie, just in case.

"Well, Chelsea, how about that?" Abby muttered, even though there was no sign of Chelsea's ghost. "Who would have thought I'd end up working with ghosts?"

She decidedly didn't think: And who would have thought Chelsea would die at only eighteen?

Sighing, Abby tore her eyes away from the house and trudged back to the car. When she was safely tucked inside, she took another sip of her drink and checked her phone.

Her mother had sent three texts: Sam's phone number, a long-winded explanation that included links to writing professional contracts, and an address of a place called 'Willow's Edge Bed and Breakfast.'

Abby dropped her phone into the empty cup holder and leaned back in the driver's seat, starting the engine. As she pulled out of the shadow of 103 Blackthorn Lane, the excitement of getting her first paid ghost-hunting gig was almost enough to drown out the hollow feeling of disappointment at being unable to contact Chelsea.

Almost.

Chapter One

It had taken some convincing to get Lucas Clark on board with a six-hour trip from their suburban Virginia town to the Connecticut coast, especially when he wasn't thrilled with their new ghost-investigation business, Spiritless. Or Spirited Away. The title was a work in progress. Whatever they called it, Lucas seemed to see it as *Abby's* ghost-investigation business, but even he had not passed up the opportunity to spend a few nights free at Willow's Edge Bed and Breakfast.

"Whoa, this town is gorgeous." Lucas whistled as Abby's car rolled to a stop in the center of a peaceful town square lightly dusted with snow. The GPS chimed that their destination would be two blocks ahead, on the left. "Is that a comic book store?"

Abby tapped her fingers against the wheel. "We can check it out after we wrap up our assignment."

Lucas turned to her, knotting his fingers together. "You brought enough salt?"

"For the hundredth time, *yes*. I brought the whole briefcase and extra salt."

"Did you test the salt gun to make sure it still works?"

Abby chewed her lip. She hadn't tested the salt gun, but it had worked fine last time, so she saw no need. The light turned green and she put her turn signal on, rolling into the left lane at a slow speed so she could make the sharp turn ahead. "Everything works."

As Abby turned the car into a pebbled driveway, a pale pink Victorian-style home loomed ahead, complete with a wrap-around porch and icing-like trim. Abby recognized it from the website even before she saw the sign that read *Willow's Edge Bed and Breakfast, circa 1860.*

"Did you know this place was listed in the top ten most romantic vacation spots in America?" Lucas sighed longingly. "If only Wanda could be here."

"I thought you broke up." Abby raised her voice as the car bounced over the pebbles.

"I know, but—if she'd just given me a little more time, I'd have found a better job and—"

Abby parked her car beside a black sedan and turned to him. "You deserve to be with someone who sees how amazing you are, no matter what you're doing. You aren't your career."

Patches of sunlight danced across his face, illuminating the worry lines in his dark brown skin. He ran a hand over his tight curls. "Thanks, Abby."

Abby grinned as she opened the car door and stepped out into the shade of a forest canopy. Cool air tingled her nose, fresh with the scent of pine. "I, for one, think you have the perfect pair of jobs."

Lucas leaned against Abby's car, shutting the door behind

him. He squinted at the house, shielding his eyes from the
sun, and skewing his glasses in the process. They were the
thin golden wide-framed pair he'd bought before grad school
because he thought they made him look like a Professor. With
the sleeves of his Spider-Man hoodie rolled up to his elbows
and his sweatpants tucked into his sneakers, he looked more
like a tired college student. But this was the most relaxed Abby
had seen him in years. She missed this laid-back side of him.

He glanced at her, chewing his lip in a way that signaled he
was nervous. "You know this is temporary, right?"

Abby moved toward the front of the car, studying him from
across the hood. "What do you mean?"

He cleared his throat, and pointedly avoided meeting her
gaze. "I took the tutoring job back home as a temporary
position. I'm going to leave it as soon as I get a real teaching
offer."

"I know."

"It could be anywhere."

A lump formed in the back of Abby's throat. "I know."

"Good." Lucas glanced apologetically at Abby, scuffing his
faded sneakers against the pebbles. "Just as long as we're on
the same page. I'm more of a consultant for this paranormal
gig. Not a business partner."

"Not a business partner, got it." Abby yanked open the back
door of her car and slid a worn leather briefcase out from
under the passenger seat. The faded bronze latches clicked
open under her fingers, releasing a familiar scent of aged
papers that tickled her nose. She fumbled through a stack
of thin journals, various packets of salt, and the antique
ghost-hunting supplies she had recently acquired when the
previous owner, Glen Ashford, had died and passed them on

to her—in that order.

When she emerged from the car, Lucas was frowning at her.

"What now?" Abby asked, the lump in her throat tightening.

"Why did you bring me?"

"Because I don't exactly want to hunt ghosts by myself."

"No, I mean, why *me*? Why not Mina?"

Oh, that. She glanced at the garden, picturing Mina on the white porch swing, her dark hair loose in the breeze, her brown eyes twinkling with mirth. There had been an undeniable connection between them at Lucas's sister's wedding last December and, when Mina had come to visit Abby shortly after the wedding, they'd grown even closer. Technically, Mina had met Abby to borrow—and then return—her binoculars and walkie-talkie, but there had been some flirting and kissing at those meetings that left Abby breathless and giddy and— *guilty*. One minute, she would be nuzzled against Mina in the back of her car, watching snowflakes drift slowly past the windshield, and the next she was thinking of how Chelsea's last moments had been looking through a windshield. Had that been what killed her? The glass? Or was it the impact?

Abby shook her head, returning her attention to Lucas. "She can't make it until Saturday."

"She's working?"

Abby nodded. "Filming ends late Friday night. There's a chance her part will be finished sooner, but they do a lot of stunt work at the end so—"

"So, it'll be another *Pal*entine's Day with the two of us." A weary smile lifted the corners of Lucas's eyes. "Just like old times."

Abby had forgotten Valentine's Day was this weekend until they had passed numerous billboards and signs advertising couples' cheese and wine tastings, jewelry sales, and chocolate festivals on their drive over. "On the way home, do you want to buy all the fifty-percent-off chocolate? We can make those super-sweet pancakes."

"You mean *I'll* be making those pancakes? All you did was lick the spoon."

"I added the chocolate!" Abby insisted, leading Lucas across the frosted grass toward the front porch.

He stuck to the gravel path, his suitcase protesting as it bounced behind him, spitting up rocks.

"Please, you ate half the chocolate chips before they made it to the batter."

Abby climbed a few creaky stairs to the front porch as the door opened.

Someone who could only be described as *incredibly gothic* stepped out. Their dark hair was swept to the side, revealing a pale face framed by thick glasses and black lipstick. Thorny tattoos peeked out from the sleeves of their uniform while skulls sneered from their boots. Abby grinned before she even saw the name tag amidst the numerous spooky pins across their vest. "Sam!"

The corners of Sam's eyes crinkled as they returned Abby's grin. They stepped into a patch of sun, which illuminated the light brown freckles along their nose. "Abby! Thank you for coming."

As Sam threw their arms around Abby in a hug, she was suddenly engulfed by their sweet musky cologne. Or perfume. Whichever it was, Abby would bet twenty bucks they'd picked it up at Hot Topic.

Lucas cleared his throat.

"Ah, Sam, you remember my friend Lucas?"

Sam turned to Lucas and squinted, before smiling a wide toothy grin. "It's been ages."

"It has," Lucas agreed stiffly.

"The last time I saw you, you were upset Abby and I went to get bubble tea without you," Sam said lightly. "When was that? About four years ago?"

Lucas's eyebrows knitted together. "I was upset because Abby challenged the Marshall brothers to a basketball game—two on two—and then left me midgame to deal with them alone."

Abby gave an apologetic shrug as Sam turned back to the house.

"So," Sam said, scratching the back of their head, "should I show you to your room or do you want a tour of this place? I'm not really sure how this works."

"Rooms first," Abby suggested. "We can drop off our luggage, get our equipment set up, and then start the tour from there."

"Sounds good. I'm stiff from being in the car all day." Lucas rolled his shoulder in an exaggerated motion.

"Right this way." Sam gestured inside.

Lucas started forward, but his suitcase jolted him back. He carried it inside and knelt beside it, his brow furrowing as he examined the wheels.

Abby stepped around him, entering the warm makeshift lobby that faced a grand open staircase, with numerous doors on each side and a small concierge podium directly ahead. Beside it, a golden retriever lay sprawled across a plush red cushion, snoring gently. Outdated floral wallpaper adorned the walls, its faded patterns surprisingly charming between aged oil paintings and modern Valentine's Day decor.

A pair of armchairs with red blankets and heart-shaped

cushions rested to Abby's right, creating the hint of a romantic waiting area, but her attention was drawn to her left, where a small cardboard display stood encircled by books and trinkets. A grainy black-and-white photo of a pale blonde teenage girl rested in the center of the display. Abby didn't even need to scan the titles of the various books and keepsakes. With their dark gothic outlines and misty silhouettes, they screamed 'haunted.'

The door to Abby's left opened and she barely stepped out of the way in time to avoid being hit in the face as a gray-haired man rushed past, his vision half obscured by a large cardboard box.

The man walked straight into Lucas, who was still kneeling on the ground, having removed a small rock from the back wheel of his suitcase.

He barely bumped him, but they both cried in alarm as if ambushed. The man dropped his box with a start and whirled around, staring at Lucas as if he were some sort of intruder— or, perhaps, a ghost.

"Sorry," Lucas mumbled, squinting as he fumbled with his glasses, which had slipped off his face. He had somehow managed to catch them before they crashed to the floor.

The golden retriever barked, running toward the commotion with his tail wagging in an enthusiastic greeting.

"Down, Cupid!" Sam called as he nearly knocked Lucas over.

Lucas adjusted his glasses and cautiously patted Cupid's head.

"He's really sweet," Sam assured him.

"If you don't mind being slobbered all over," the man added, massaging his shoulder as if it pained him.

Abby studied the stranger as his scowl deepened. Despite

him wearing the same uniform as Sam, the two looked like they had stepped out of different film sets. While Sam could have starred in *The Addams Family*, this guy looked like he could blend right into the background of a large corporate advertisement. His uniform was completely plain: black collared shirt, matching trousers, red vest, and worn practical shoes. He wore nothing personal—no pins, watch, or wedding ring—nothing but his name tag that read 'Harvey.' Wrinkles framed his weary eyes and he slouched as if some great weight pressed against his shoulders. He gave Abby the impression of a deeply unhappy man, who had spent many years suffering and was resigned to it.

Abby recognized the weight of grief. She had seen it in the mirror for years after Chelsea's death. She wondered who or what this man had lost to make him so cold and abrasive.

"Let me help with that." Abby knelt beside him, picked up a fallen towel, and put it back in the box.

Shaking their head, Sam took the towel and folded it neatly on the podium before returning it to the box.

"Young people these days," the man grumbled, clumsily folding a towel. "You've no respect for your elders. Always in such a hurry."

"These are the friends I was telling you about," Sam said brightly. "My cousin, Abby, and her ghost-hunting partner, Lucas."

"Technically, I'm a consultant," Lucas muttered.

"Ghost hunters, huh?" Harvey's eyes flashed between Abby and the display in the window.

"I like to think of us more as paranormal investigators," Abby corrected. "Ghosts aren't always dangerous, and we don't hunt them."

"We're more like ghost agents," Lucas added. "Helping them complete their unfinished business so they can move on."

Harvey shook his head as if he couldn't believe what he was hearing. "I've got to take these towels upstairs."

"We've got it." Sam's rings clinked as they made thumbs-up signs with both hands. "Which rooms?"

"Violet and Magnolia." Harvey grunted once more before turning and opening a door labeled 'Staff Only.' Abby caught a glimpse of a small office cramped with antique furniture before the door shut.

"He's not very pleasant," Abby commented.

"That's Harvey for you." Sam picked up the box of towels and rested it on their hip. "He's one of the new hires. He acts cranky, but I think he's just lonely. If I worked in hospitality for fifty years, I'd be cranky too."

Lucas winced as Cupid's pink tongue licked the back of his hand. "Is this your dog?"

"Technically, he's Nathan's." Sam shrugged. "Nathan owns this place. But he's hardly ever around anymore and I've been taking care of Cupid since I started working here, so he said I could have him. I just haven't signed the paperwork yet."

"How old is he?" Abby kneeled beside Lucas and Cupid promptly greeted her, pawing her outstretched hand.

"He just turned one," Sam said fondly, starting up a steep set of stairs. "Stay, Cupid."

Cupid obediently returned to his bed and circled it twice, before taking a seat with his ears tilted upward as if he was waiting for the next interesting thing to call to him.

The front door opened once more and a tall, thin woman hurried in, her dark heels clicking loudly on the polished floor.

Beaded sunflower earrings dangled from her ears as she pulled her bleached blonde hair into a ponytail with one hand, her other gripping a bright tumbler. "Sorry, I'm late! Car trouble."

"Again?" Sam called without turning to face her. "The kitchen is ready for you."

The woman nodded, pausing to sip her drink, and leaving a bright red lipstick stain on her tumbler. Unlike Harvey, everything about this woman magnified her vibrant personality. Abby suspected she was an artist, of some sort. The flowers on the tumbler were well painted but slightly smeared, her earrings subtly different in size, and her beaded necklace had an occasional break in the pattern. She either made most of these accessories herself or was close to someone who had made them. She soon disappeared into the living room, the double doors swinging shut behind her.

"That's Susan, the waitress. Well, I guess she's now the cook too," Sam explained, moving down the second-floor landing. "It's a miracle we ever serve dinner on time."

"She must be good if she got promoted," Lucas commented.

"Sure." Sam snorted. "Or Nathan just likes her."

They stopped in front of a door marked *Magnolia* and knocked on the polished wood. When there was no response, they twisted the delicate brass handle. The door squeaked open into a charming vintage room, complete with an iron bed and lace curtains, that could only be described as *pink*.

Pink carnation wallpaper ran from floor to ceiling, hidden only by rosy trim and the occasional framed photo. Even the furniture was overwhelmingly pink. Thankfully, someone had wisely made the bedspread and loveseat a contrasting blue, but that wasn't enough to balance the sea of pink.

Abby started to follow Sam inside, but they shook their head.

"Yours is two floors up. I'm just dropping off the towels."

"Who's Magnolia Wentworth?" Lucas asked, reading the plaque outside the door.

"One of the original owners. Her husband, Charles, was the first person born in this house. He inherited it when he was only twelve years old. The story goes he and Magnolia planned on having a big family but ended up with a single son, John. He's the one who turned this place into an inn."

Sam returned to the hall, leading them past a room labeled 'Charles' and up another flight of polished yet creaky stairs.

"Are all of the rooms named after the family?" Lucas asked.

"They are all named after notable residents. There's Charles, Magnolia, and John on the second floor. The third has Sarah Jane, Scarlett, and Violet—all memorable guests or residents of the inn at one point or another. And then the top floor is just your room—Nellie's room."

"Who was Nellie?" Abby asked as Sam slipped a key into the single white door at the top of the stairs.

"A girl who grew up here in the 1950s. One of the innkeeper's daughters. Until about thirty years ago, the innkeeper used to live here. It's pretty much a full suite, although a bit cramped. Here we are—"

Sam held the door open as Abby and Lucas stepped into a warm, cozy room. Sunlight spilled through far windows, washing the pastel walls in cheery yellow rays. To their left, a pair of twin beds faced the window, separated by a small writing desk topped with stationery and a vase of fresh flowers. To their right, a fully stocked kitchenette tempted Abby to dig into bright boxes of candy.

Lucas's eyes lit up. "This place is fantastic!"

He hurried to the kitchenette and flipped through the

various snacks, opening a box of candy hearts.

"Where do the innkeepers stay now?" Abby asked.

"There isn't one anymore, not really. Nathan only visits a few times a month, and only works around holidays when we're extra busy. Harvey, Susan, and I take care of all the day-to-day stuff. There's a chef that comes on special occasions, but Susan cooks the rest of the time."

Lucas moved to the window, peering out at the back garden while snacking on his candy hearts. "The view is—oh my god!"

"What?" Abby asked, hurrying to his side. She scanned the grounds for someone in danger, but the only person in sight was a middle-aged woman sitting on a rocking chair, reading a book, a mug of coffee on the table beside her. She hardly seemed in danger.

"Is that Dr. Catherine Greenwood?" Lucas squinted, pressing his face against the glass.

"It is," Sam confirmed. "Though I'm afraid I'll have to ask you not to bother the other guests."

"Man, oh man!" Lucas opened the window, letting in a gust of chilled air. He rested his head against the screen, grinning from ear to ear and sighing like some lead in an old-fashioned romance movie.

Abby nudged him. "Who is this woman you're being all creepy about?"

Sighing once more, Lucas shut the window and turned back to Abby. "She's a Pulitzer Prize–winning author, and the dean of the English department at Yale."

Abby couldn't tell if 'Pulitzer Prize winner' was an actual great achievement, or something only Lucas knew about. Either way, he sounded impressed. "She sounds perfect for you—are you going to ask her out?"

Horror flashed across Lucas's face. "Don't be ridiculous. She's twice my age." He lowered his voice, holding his hand up in a way that blocked Sam from reading his lips, but made it very clear he was whispering something behind their back. "I'm going to ask her for a job."

"Ooh." Abby nodded, knowing how much Lucas wanted to get a job teaching at a university. She thought he'd applied to all of them by now. Apparently not.

"Speaking of jobs," Sam said, making it clear that Lucas's whispering hadn't been as quiet as he had intended, "your uniforms are in the closet."

"What uniforms?" Lucas asked.

"For cleaning." Sam blinked. "Didn't Abby tell you?"

Lucas shot Abby an accusatory glance. "She didn't say anything about cleaning."

"Because it's not important," Abby said, waving a hand. "You won't have to do much of it. We have someone coming Friday morning to deep clean before the weekend. Just pick up the dirty towels and sheets and place them in one of these—" they held up a laundry bag "—which you can bring to the front office. Harvey and I will take it from there."

Lucas made a *tsk* sound of disapproval. "I should have known there was a catch to this place. No way we get paid to stay here."

"Well, the cleaning is just a cover to get you access to their rooms," Sam explained. "So you can communicate with the ghost."

Chapter Two

"How dangerous is this ghost?" Lucas asked, inspecting an electric kettle that rested in a small kitchenette.

"Harmless. Nothing compared to the last one." Abby ran her hands over a patchwork quilt at the foot of the bed. The stitching had come undone in places, and several of the patches had faded with age.

Lucas's hand wrapped around Abby's, pulling her back. "Don't touch that!"

Abby gave him a curious glance. "Why?"

"Because it's old!" He waved his hand, returning to the kitchenette, where he filled the kettle with water. "Number one rule of ghost hunting, don't touch creepy old things."

"Everything in this place is old," Sam muttered, checking their phone. "And I wouldn't say our ghost is harmless. We've had half a dozen guests leave early, scared to death. We can't keep anyone working here for more than a few weeks. I'm the only one who's been here more than six months."

Abby moved further up the bed, taking a seat on the plush white duvet. The mattress squeaked, loud and high-pitched, making her wince.

"It better not do that all night," Lucas said, reaching for a powdered donut.

"Wait!" Sam lunged toward him.

Lucas stiffened. "What's wrong? Has it been poisoned?"

Sam gently moved Lucas aside, straightened the box of donuts, and crouched, holding their phone toward the kitchenette. They snapped a few pictures, then straightened. "Sorry. The lighting was bad earlier."

"The lighting…on the donuts?" Lucas's eyebrows furrowed.

"Yep," Sam replied without looking up from their phone. "Treats do well on social media this time of year. Don't know why. Probably when people are ready to start breaking their New Year's resolutions?"

Lucas slowly reached toward the donuts, eyeing Sam as if he thought they might lunge at him again any second. When he had successfully secured a powdered donut on a napkin, he turned back to Sam. "Why haven't you quit?"

Sam shrugged, slipping their phone into their back pocket. "It's a nice job. And I've never really felt in danger. At first, some guests complained about the water acting weird, small objects moving around their room—I thought they were just trying to scam us into a refund. But the stories got odder, and more frequent—lights turning on and off in the middle of the night, words written on the window, mysterious footsteps in the walls. I thought it was a prank. I just couldn't figure out who would do it, or why. And then there was the incident with Nakita."

The electric kettle hummed as the water boiled.

Sensing a story, Abby leaned in closer and prompted, "What incident?"

Sam's face paled. They twisted a dark studded earring. "It was night, just over a week ago—I was in the lobby, getting ready to lock up for the evening and head home, when I heard her scream. She was on the second floor, running toward the stairs like—well, like she'd seen a ghost."

Abby leaned further forward, the hair on her arms rising in anticipation. "Then what?"

"She fell down the stairs, knocked herself out. Scared me to death. I had to call an ambulance. She's okay—thank god—but she broke her arm and had a mild concussion. It wasn't until the paramedics cleared out and the guests settled down that I saw the ashes."

"Ashes?" Lucas's voice hitched.

Sam nodded. Though they kept their voice steady, Abby could see the tremor in their shoulders. They were trying hard to look unfazed. "Yep. They were smeared across the far wall in Violet. I nearly jumped out of my skin when I saw them. They spelled out 'Don't Forget.'"

"Don't forget," Abby echoed. "Don't forget what?"

"Her death." Sam let out a shaky breath. "She doesn't want us to forget her death."

"Who?" Lucas asked.

"Violet Lovelace."

The kettle clicked off with a note of finality. Lucas jumped. He poured the steaming water into two mugs, sticking a tea bag in one and dumping a packet of hot chocolate in the other. "Is she the one with the creepy photo downstairs?"

Abby recalled the woman staring out from the haunted history display as Sam nodded and explained, "Legend has it, she's been haunting this place for fifty years, ever since she died in a fire in 1975."

"How old was she?" Abby asked, unable to shake the feeling of how young the woman looked in the picture.

"Eighteen. Poor girl died before she could even order a drink," Sam attempted to joke.

The joke fell flat as Lucas shook his head and Abby gave a sharp intake of breath. Pain flared in her heart. Violet had died at the same age as Chelsea.

"How did the fire start?" asked Lucas.

"The kitchen. At the Valentine's Day party. She was working as a server when she saw the fire. She warned everyone but was unable to get out herself. Some say she went back in for a secret recipe, or money she had stashed away. Others say she trapped herself inside, sacrificing herself to contain the fire. But all we know for sure is that she never made it out."

Abby shuddered.

Lucas handed her the mug of hot chocolate. "And you think her ghost doesn't want to be forgotten?"

Sam ran their fingers through their hair. "Maybe. Susan thinks she's out for vengeance, chastising guests for vacationing on her grave. Harvey suspects the ghost is upset we're bringing back the Valentine's Day dinner. I don't know what to think. I'm not sure I even believe in ghosts."

Lucas's jaw dropped. Abby could see his gaze taking in Sam's black nail polish, skull accessories, and morbid pins. "*You* don't believe in ghosts?"

"What can I say?" Sam shrugged. "I'm a person of science."

"Sam's a former chemist," Abby said, breathing in the velvety scent of her hot chocolate. She took a sip and let out a satisfied sigh.

Lucas's eyes widened. "You left *chemistry* to manage the front desk at a hotel?"

"And their social media. And their finances. Hell, I practically run this whole place. It's a huge upgrade from working in a lab all day with grouchy old men who have no respect for anyone who doesn't look like them. Did Abby tell you about the time they told me my glasses were 'too distracting'?"

Abby cleared her throat. The only person who could get off track even more easily than she could was Sam. "What else can you tell us about Violet?"

"That's it." Sam moved to the radiator and turned up the heat. It groaned to life with a soft rattling sound. When Sam returned, they moved closer to Abby and gestured for Lucas to step closer as well. "If you find anything, can you record it? You wouldn't think there's a market in hauntings, but those *Haunted History* books sell like hotcakes. If we could get some real footage of a ghost, we could draw in a crowd."

Lucas's brow furrowed. "I thought you didn't believe in ghosts."

"I said I'm not sure if I believe in ghosts or not. You get me the proof, and I'll make my decision." Sam scratched the back of their neck. "Although, it'd be best if you could get her rattling the windows or something harmless. Don't mess with the guests."

"I'm not sure we can control a ghost." Abby got the sinking suspicion that Sam might think this was one of Abby's theatrics and that the 'ghosts' she vanquished were nothing more than sheets and illusions.

Sam shrugged off her response. "I've got a camera installed outside Violet. Maybe it could just float past there?"

"You didn't put a camera inside the room?" Lucas asked.

"Isn't that where the ashes showed up?"

"We've got guests in there. I don't want to break any privacy laws and I do *not* want to see what they do alone in bed."

Lucas rubbed the edge of his glasses. "If you don't believe in ghosts, then how do you explain what's been going on?"

Sam jerked a thumb toward the window. "The Spring Meadow Inn. It opened about two years ago. They had a great opening, better than this place. There's not much to do in this small town. We're too far from the coast and too far from the city for most folks. We target the 'peaceful countryside getaway' crowd. The inn has more accessible rooms than us, so they get most of the retired folks. Part of why I was hired was to do the marketing—they want to appeal to a younger crowd. We added all sorts of romantic packages—young couples, newlywed discounts, and the like. Since most of our appeal revolves around romance, Valentine's Day seems like the perfect opportunity to draw people in."

"You think Spring Meadow Inn is jealous?"

"Could be," Sam admitted. "They offered me a job right before all this started and I turned them down. I don't mean to brag, but our bookings have nearly tripled since I joined the team. It's all about the special events. We slayed Halloween and Christmas, and our ceremonial Valentine's Day dinner is sold out—we even added extra tables."

Lucas rubbed his chin. "So you start doing better than the Inn—they start a rumor this place is haunted to scare people away—"

"And back to them," Sam concluded. "I know it's a bit far-fetched, but the timing adds up. The first haunting was right before our Christmas Dinner—another event that sold out and made newsworthy headlines. The cook showed up to the kitchen and found that someone had written across a wall in chalk: 'Don't you know this place is a tomb?' I thought it was just some kid doing some poetic graffiti or something, but then the messages kept popping up. I heard about you trying to start a paranormal investigation agency, so I thought—what the hell? Maybe it really is a ghost. Maybe you can get to the bottom of this."

"You bet we can," Abby declared, standing with an exaggerated stretch. "Give us twenty-four hours and we'll tell you if it's Violet or not."

Sam nodded. "Let me know if there's anything I can help with."

"Will do. Do all of the hauntings take place in certain areas? Or are they all over?"

"All over." Sam paused, twisting their earring. "Well, the messages have appeared in the Violet room, the Charles room, the kitchen, and outside."

"Do you have a list of every message?"

"I have pictures. I can text them to you." Sam began scrolling through their phone. "The only one I don't have is from Christmas—the same night the first message appeared, Nakita said she was cleaning up when she heard a voice whisper, 'I'm back. I won't let you go this time.'"

"Well, that's ominous," said Abby.

Lucas flung open the door. "That's my cue to leave."

Abby grabbed his arm, pulling him back inside. "Oh, come on, you were so excited to stay here. Besides, she could have been exaggerating. Or making it up, if Sam's theory is true. Let's just take a look around and see what we can find."

Abby's phone pinged as a series of Sam's texts came through, image thumbnails attached.

Sam tucked their phone back into their pocket. "Please wear the uniforms if you go into any guest rooms, and make sure you knock first. Don't leave anything behind that could interfere with their stay."

"No cameras in the guest rooms," Abby said. "Got it."

"Or messes," Sam added.

Abby nodded. "The place will be spotless, promise."

After a quick exchange of goodbyes, Sam departed and Abby locked the door behind them. A quick sweep of the room with her binoculars showed several layers of aged wallpaper and wisps of long-gone furniture, but no ghosts. "We're alone."

"Good." Lucas reached for his bags. "We've got time to get out of here."

"Relax, this ghost isn't trying to kill anyone."

"Yet," Lucas added under his breath.

Abby pulled up the images Sam had texted her. There were four:

> **Don't you know this place is a tomb?** in white chalk across the kitchen wall
>
> **Don't Forget** in ashes across purple floral wallpaper
>
> **Ready to Join Me?** in lipstick on an oval mirror
>
> ...*to my grave* had been added to a former welcome sign on the front door, again in white chalk, transforming it into a sinister greeting: **Welcome to my grave.**

Abby passed her phone to Lucas. "It seems like Violet is just scaring people with her creepy messages, but she's not actually hurting anyone. We already know who our culprit is. All we need to do is figure out what's keeping her here and send her on. Easy-peasy."

A shriek rose from the hall. Shrill and panicked, it made the hair on Abby's neck rise as she jumped to her feet and reached for the door.

"Don't," Lucas pleaded, backing away from the door.

Abby turned the knob and stepped out into the hall.

Sunlight drifted through the windows, revealing a thin layer of dust at the edge of their sills. The shriek kept repeating itself like an alarm, rising up from the floor below, making the floor tremble.

Abby recognized the source immediately. A tall middle-aged woman stood alone on the burgundy carpet, a white towel wrapped around her, her long blonde hair hanging loose down her back. It was dry, as was her skin, meaning whatever she had seen had likely occurred just before she had gotten into the shower or bath.

"What's wrong?" Abby asked, running downstairs. She stopped beside the woman on the third-floor landing as the screaming subsided to a choked sob.

The woman shook her head, pointing to an open door down the hall. The Violet room.

"Hello?" Abby called, opening the door wider.

A cheery pastel room greeted her, complete with floral wallpaper that Abby recognized from one of Sam's pictures. All signs of the ash had been cleared, and the thin purple flowers shone in sunlight. Frost crept across the far windows. In the adjoining bathroom, water splashed against the ceramic tub in a steady shower.

"Is anyone here?" Abby took a tentative step deeper into the room, slipping the binoculars from her backpack. As she raised them to her eyes, the shower came fully into view, separated from the rest of the room only by a thin pane of frosted glass and an open doorway.

The shower was empty.

No humans, no ghosts.

The mirror showed only her own reflection, blurred by steam, and an ominous message revealed in the condensation: *You Sleep on Bones.*

Lucas's hesitant footsteps pattered across the carpet as he joined her. "Easy-peasy, huh?"

Abby considered that she may have misspoken. Perhaps they were dealing with a more sinister spirit than they had anticipated. She recalled the first time she had been attacked by a ghost, the feeling of icy fingers pressing against her throat, making it impossible to breathe. She shook the thought. If there was a malicious spirit here, they would send it on. After all, that's what she planned on making her career out of. Who would hire a ghost hunter who ran at the first sign of danger?

Shaking her head, Abby slipped out her phone and snapped a picture of the writing on the mirror, mentally adding it to the list of haunted messages Sam had sent. This mirror lacked the bronze frame of the mirror that had contained the message drawn in lipstick, but that was two messages on mirrors and two messages in this particular room. After confirming the image was clear, she pocketed her phone and moved to the bed, crouching beside it.

"What are you doing?" Lucas's voice hitched with concern.

"Checking for bones." Finding nothing under the bed, Abby stood and peeled back the sheets. They were bone-free as well.

"I think it's metaphorical," Lucas said. "Violet died here, and people are sleeping 'over her bones' even if they're technically buried somewhere else."

"Where was she buried?" Abby asked, curious.

"In a graveyard a few blocks from here."

"And you know this, how?"

"I looked it up?"

"When?"

"A few minutes ago."

Abby bit back a grin. "No, you didn't. You haven't taken your phone out."

"Fine," Lucas admitted. "I may have done some research before we got here."

"I knew it! You *like* paranormal investigating."

"I *like* being prepared," Lucas said with an exasperated sigh as they returned to the hall.

The woman in the towel was now sobbing on the shoulder of a middle-aged man who—considering their matching wedding bands—was likely her husband. Harvey stood a few feet away trying (and failing) to comfort them. Sam stood in the doorway, frowning.

Abby took a deep breath and declared boldly, "I want this room for the night."

Chapter Three

Dusk crept in, casting a golden glow across Abby's ghost-hunting supplies, which cluttered the antique desk, and gleamed off the pins on her overstuffed messenger bag.

"You're sure you want to spend the night here?"

Abby nodded. Her request had been easily granted after the previous occupants demanded a refund and sent Harvey to gather their things before they moved to the Spring Meadow Inn. Something Lucas had made it clear he wished to do as well.

"I've got salt." Abby pointed to the ring of salt coating the floor around the bed. "Violet can't hurt me. I just want to talk to her. See if I can figure out why she's doing this."

"And what's keeping her here," Lucas reminded Abby. "This vacation will get a whole lot better the moment I don't have to worry about ghosts attacking in my sleep."

"You can do that tonight. You know salt stops them."

"Weakens them," Lucas corrected.

"Same thing."

"Uh, no, that is not the same thing. Not at all."

Abby's phone rang. Mina's name flashed across the screen and her stomach knotted with mixed emotions. She couldn't help but picture Mina here, leaning against the luxurious bed, smirking at the lavish wallpaper, her eyes crinkling in amusement. The back of her neck prickled at the thought, as if someone was in her mind, judging her for thinking such things. As if *Chelsea* was judging her.

Shoving thoughts of her former girlfriend aside, Abby answered the phone as cheerily as she could manage. "Hey, you."

"Hey yourself," Mina replied. "How goes the ghost hunting?"

"Is that Mina?" Lucas asked.

"Hang on." Abby shooed Lucas into the hall, draping the binoculars around his neck and handing him a box of salt.

"It's Mina, isn't it? Tell her I say hi—"

Abby shut the door in his face, resuming her attention to Mina. "Sorry about that."

Mina's amused laughter rang through in its usual melodic way, bringing butterflies to Abby's stomach.

"Where were we?"

"I was asking how the ghost hunting was going."

"Hasn't really started yet." Abby glanced at the mirror, where the message had gleamed several minutes ago. Now, it only showed her reflection—not even a streak of grease. Lucas had done well.

The sound of distant traffic and rustling fabric came through the other line. Mina sounded the way she usually did when commuting to and from work—brisk and focused, with the occasional 'excuse me,' '*can you not?*,' or similar interruption. "Since Lucas is still there, I take it there hasn't been any danger?"

"No, just creepy messages."

"What sort of creepy messages?" Mina's voice tightened, a note of concern slipping through.

"Something about tombs, bones, death—the usual."

"I didn't know we had a 'usual' for these things."

"Yeah, well, what can I say? Apparently, ghosts think a lot about death." Abby leaned against the headboard, twisting the button on her sweater. She imagined the smirk playing across Mina's lips, and the feel of those lips against hers. "I wish you were here."

The words slipped out before she had thought through the full impact they would have. Her heartbeat quickened, her stomach tight with nerves. Right now, with their virtual dates, late-night phone calls, and movie nights, it was like having a fictional girlfriend. Someone to share life with, without having to get too close—physically or emotionally. But picturing her here—her strong arms wrapped around Abby, the scent of her nutty shampoo against the pillows—made Abby's heart race with fear and desire.

"I miss you too," Mina's soft response crackled through the phone.

The fear subsided a little, as Abby's stomach began to summersault with joy and longing.

"Ah, hell, I was going to surprise—"

The door shook as someone pounded on it from the other side.

"Abby!" Lucas called in a loud whisper between panicked breaths. "Abby!"

"Hold that thought," Abby said, dropping the phone on the bed. She opened the door and found Lucas shoving the binoculars into her hands, pointing at the opposite end of the hall.

"Did you see her?" Abby asked excitedly.

Lucas shook his head, his hand trembling.

Abby frowned. "Then what?"

Lucas cupped her hands around the binoculars and raised them to her eyes. Through them, Abby watched the hall transform into a shadow of what it had been decades ago, the ghosts of pictures long lost hung askew over one another as decades crammed into one image. And there, at the end of the hall, an old man sat in the ghost of a rocking chair. His striped pajamas trailed past his bare feet and his nightcap slipped so low it nearly fell off the back of his head. He scowled at Abby, mouthing something she couldn't make out.

"The walkie-talkie," she whispered. She dashed back into the Violet room and riffled through her supplies until she found the device.

It crackled to life as she strolled back into the hall.

"Ah, she returns," the ghost said, then started, seemingly surprised to hear his own voice echoing through the static. "Golly, can you hear me with that thing?"

Abby nodded, clipping the walkie-talkie to her front pocket and raising the binoculars. Sam hadn't mentioned any old men haunting the hotel. She had naively assumed Violet was the only ghost. It occurred to her briefly that Violet might not even be a ghost at all, but that this man had been acting in her name.

She needed to start doing her own research instead of taking the word of people who didn't even believe in ghosts.

The ghost clapped his hands together. "Splendid. I've been

dying for a cup of coffee. Or better yet, do you play croquet?"

"Uh, not really." Abby studied the man through the binoculars. Despite gray hair and wrinkles, his eyes glinted with joy over a boyish grin. He was either genuinely eager for their attention or completely unhinged and toying with them. His baggy pajamas and bare feet amplified both options.

"A shame." The ghost's expression fell for a moment, then brightened. "I can teach you. There's a set in the attic. They used to bring it down every summer, but they haven't touched it in years—or decades, I suppose. Time sure does fly when you're dead."

Abby felt a touch of relief at his words—having previously encountered a spirit oblivious of his current deathly state, she was glad to avoid that experience again.

"What's your name?" Abby asked.

"Charles. Charles Wentworth. What's yours?"

"Abby. Abby Spector, and this is my friend, Lucas Clark."

Lucas raised his hand in an awkward half-wave, half-frightened motion.

"Let me guess, you two are here to write a story on Violet."

Abby and Lucas exchanged glances. If he knew about Violet, that meant her ghost was probably still around.

"What makes you say that?" Abby asked.

Charles leaned back, a smug grin on his face. "You aren't the first mediums to come here."

"We aren't mediums," Lucas said, glancing up from typing notes in his phone. "We're paranormal investigators."

"Every year it's fancy new terms and fancy new gadgets." Charles shook his head. "I'm just glad we're past 'tap twice if you can hear me'—of course I can hear you! Stop waking me up by banging on the walls. Ghosts sleep too, you know. But we don't dream. It's nice. Peaceful."

"I didn't know that," Abby admitted, making a mental note to add it to her notebook where she recorded all she knew about the mechanics of ghosts. "Why would we want to write about Violet?"

Charles shrugged. "She's the most famous, most interesting of the lot of us. They've got that whole shrine to her downstairs. Not sure why. Think it's the broken heart, the longing, early death—all the makings of a good story. No one wants to read about a sixty-eight-year-old man who lived a full life and died in his sleep."

"Does that disappoint you?" Abby asked cautiously. "Do you wish they paid more attention to you?"

Charles shook his head. "Hell no, I couldn't care less what you all think of me. I just want some peace and quiet around here. And tell whoever's in charge to bring the croquet back. I'd love to watch a game."

"You wouldn't happen to know anything about who is terrorizing the guests, would you?"

Lucas elbowed her for her lack of tact, but she was able to see the genuine surprise and confusion flash across Charles's face at her question. "What do you mean?"

"Someone's been sneaking into Violet's room and writing scary messages."

Charles's frown deepened. "What sort of messages?"

"Ominous threatening messages."

"Don't you know this place is a tomb," Lucas repeated the messages from memory. "Don't forget. Ready to join me? Welcome to my grave. You sleep on my bones."

Abby was already studying Charles through the binoculars. Wrinkles creased his forehead as he stared in the direction of the Violet room.

"Charles?" Abby prompted.

The ghost shook his head. "I don't know anything about any messages."

"Do you know who might?"

Charles rubbed his finger over a hint of a mustache. "Doesn't sound like Violet. Or Matilda."

"Who's Matilda?" Abby asked.

"My granddaughter, though I died before she was born."

"John's daughter?" Lucas speculated, typing faster.

Charles shook his head. "My daughter, Bethany, was her mother."

"You had a daughter?" Lucas raised an eyebrow. "Sam didn't mention that."

"I think I know my own family better than whoever Sam is."

"Fair," Abby agreed. "Did you have any other children?"

"Just the two. John had three kids—one son, two daughters. All respectable people who lived great lives, or so I'm told. As for Bethany, well—there's a reason she's not remembered."

"And that would be?" Abby asked, unable to keep the anticipation from her voice.

"Tod Burke," Charles spat. "She married that fool against my wishes. He turned out to be a real piece of work. They were only married two years before she showed up back here, pregnant with Matilda, that drunk of a husband having run off with some younger girl. Poor Bethany."

"I thought you said you died before Matilda was born?" Abby dodged Lucas's attempt at elbowing her again.

"I did, just a few days after Bethany returned home. But I'm still here in a fashion, as you can see. I don't have much memory of those years—it just comes in flashes like a dream.

Matilda playing croquet, running up and down the halls in her yellow dress, throwing her dolls off the banister."

"Sounds like me as a kid," Abby said dreamily, wishing she had grown up in a house like this instead of her parents' modern townhouse. Of course, her mother would have probably hovered around, scolding her every time she breathed too close to something valuable.

"She was spirited, I'll give her that. Had a nasty temper but a kind heart under it all. Like her mother, she fell hard for someone in town. I can't say much about the boy, one way or another. If he ever came around here, I never saw him, but it was obvious Matilda was lovestruck. She was always walking around humming lovesongs and giggling with her friends. One day, she came home all sad and depressed. Wouldn't tell us what happened, but I noticed she had a ring in a box that she never put on her finger. Shortly after, she got the flu. Went to sleep one night and didn't wake up."

Abby considered the possibilities of the ring in the box. She imagined Matilda accepting a proposal only to discover her boyfriend had been cheating on her. Or perhaps she had stumbled upon it while he was away and suspected he planned to propose to someone else.

"Do you have any idea who the boyfriend was?"

Charles let out a heavy sigh. "She wouldn't tell me. I think her mother knew. Her spirit stuck around long enough to make amends with Matilda, but she's been gone for ages now."

"Is it just the three of you?" Lucas asked. "Violet, Matilda, and you?"

Charles nodded. "Others have come and gone, but not in a long time. I like it this way. Peaceful."

Abby had to agree, this was a peaceful place to haunt.

With its hardwood floors, grand windows, and cozy furniture it created a museum-like vibe. Abby couldn't imagine any raging parties or rambunctious children in this space. From the lobby, brochures, and website, Abby got the sense most of the guests were couples looking for a relaxing getaway to enjoy the scenery. In spring, the garden probably filled with blossoms and birdsong, while in fall, the trees must transform into gorgeous shades of red and orange. She turned her attention back to Charles and asked, "What can you tell us about Violet?"

"Not much," he said. "She keeps to herself. Seems sad and melancholy. She mostly roams the gardens."

"Thanks," said Abby, making a mental note to check the gardens next. "I think that's all for now. We'll probably be back later with more questions."

"Perhaps I can answer them over a game of croquet." Charles's face softened with a smile. "I hope you find your miscreant. Don't be too hard on the girls if it turns out to be one of them."

"I'll keep that in mind," Abby said, lowering the binoculars. She shut off the walkie-talkie, saving the battery, and turned to Lucas. "Well, what do you think?"

"I think we should go to the Inn. I don't want that man watching me sleep."

Abby frowned, returning to Violet. A quick view of the room through the binoculars made it clear it was ghost-free. "I think he was telling the truth. He doesn't seem like he wants to hurt—or scare—anyone."

"He nearly scared the skin off of me. Sneaking up on me like that." Lucas shivered. "Sorry I interrupted your call. I thought you'd want to talk to him."

Abby's chest tightened with guilt as she suddenly remembered Mina. She reached for her phone and saw the lock screen, signaling the call had ended. Across it, a single text glowed: *Mina: Going to bed. Good night! Catch up tomorrow.*

The kiss emoji at the end warmed Abby's heart, though it increased her feeling of guilt. She sighed. "I'm no good at this."

"At ghost hunting?"

At dating, Abby wanted to say, but she buried her face in a pillow instead.

"You saved Mrs. Kensington, didn't you? I'm not going on record saying this, but as far as ghost investigating goes, you're pretty good at it."

"You think so?"

"Best I've seen."

Abby lifted her head to frown at him. "You haven't seen any paranormal investigators besides me."

"And myself. And Glen."

Abby felt a smile tug at her features. She may not be able to untangle the mess of feelings around Mina right now or come up with a plan for how to address that, but she was a step closer to solving this case. Clutching the binoculars to her chest, Abby moved to the window and brushed aside the lace curtains.

Dim lights illuminated a small garden winding between tables, pathways, and iron benches. A fountain bubbled quietly in the center of a stone pond, moonlight gleaming off the surface. Behind it, under a naked branch, a white porch swing rocked back and forth.

Almost like someone was swinging on it.

A peek through the binoculars confirmed her suspicions.

On the painted wood sat a young woman with blonde hair pulled into a ponytail topped with a black ribbon. She wore what could only have been her uniform—a ruby dress with a white collar and matching apron. Her feet, snug in simple black shoes, were tucked tucked casually beside her as she leaned back, looking up at the stars.

She looked young. And a little like—Chelsea. Abby's heart stung with the thought as her mind opened the floodgates of all things Chelsea. Chelsea had once been Abby's age, and now she was left behind, forever eighteen. She tried to picture the outfit Chelsea had died in and realized with gut-wrenching guilt that she didn't know. She hadn't seen Chelsea that day, before or after the accident. The funeral had been closed casket. In the portrait they displayed for her, Chelsea wore a simple black shirt, which was all wrong. Chelsea loved colors. She had probably been wearing a seafoam green blouse or floral tank top.

"What is it?" Lucas whispered, jolting her back to the present. "Do you see someone?"

Abby hurried out of the room and down the steps, rushing toward the back door. Flinging it open, she was met with chilly air heavy with pine and a faint hint of wood smoke. She shivered as it brushed her lungs. Wishing she had brought her jacket, Abby tucked her hands deeper into the sleeves of her sweater as a porch light flickered on, casting her own shadow across the iron tables. She cautiously navigated between empty chairs until she reached a stone path that led toward the swing. Still swaying, its pale exterior gleamed like a beacon against the dark snowy garden.

Abby approached cautiously. The fountain's burbling

grew louder, mingling with the wind's howl through needled branches. A quick check through the binoculars showed Violet perched on the edge of her seat, watching Abby with apprehension like a cat observing a stranger—her posture was curious, though tense as if ready to flee.

"Hi, Violet," Abby whispered, activating the walkie-talkie. Though the ghosts could hear her without it, she didn't want to miss Violet's reply. "I just want to talk."

At the sound of her name, Violet glanced up. A look of confusion and curiosity flashed across her face.

A dog barked. Abby stiffened. It sounded close.

By the time she had glanced over her shoulder, Cupid was bounding toward her waist, shoving his nose into the palm of her hand. Sniffing for treats, no doubt.

"Hi there, buddy." Abby laughed as the dog's tongue tickled her palm. She sank to her knees, scratching gently behind the dog's ear. His tail wagged vigorously.

Something crashed into Abby's side.

She jumped, frightened, before realizing it was only the bench swing.

Letting her hand fall from her heart, she took a deep breath to steady herself. The bench creaked and rattled as it continued to straighten out as if someone solid had just left its surface.

Abby returned the binoculars to her eyes.

Violet was gone.

Cupid let out a slow pleading whine as he pawed at Abby's side, and she resumed scratching behind his ear.

This hadn't gone as Abby had hoped, but she had learned two things: Violet Lovelace's spirit was still here, and she was strong enough to interact with the living world. If she could make the swing sway, she could easily have written those messages.

Abby settled onto the swing, waiting for Violet's return. Cupid snuggled by her feet, resting his paws against her sneakers. It was going to be a long night.

Chapter Four

There was nothing like waking up to a stack of waffles with whipped cream and chocolate chips. Technically, Abby had been awake for over an hour, but it wasn't until she was snuggled into a booth at the local diner with a glass of orange juice and a delicious breakfast spread out before her that she felt her full mental capacity returning.

"Did you get any sleep last night?" Lucas asked as he meticulously sliced his avocado toast into bite-sized pieces.

Abby grimaced. She had gone to bed late, having waited a few more hours for Violet to return, with no luck. When she'd finally retreated to her room and fallen asleep, she had woken frequently from dreams of Violet transforming into Chelsea and screaming accusations at her for moving on while leaving her behind, or worse—breaking down into regret-filled tears.

Abby shrugged. "A bit. You?"

Lucas nodded. "I was prepared to draw all night, thinking there was no way I'd fall asleep, but the moment my head touched that pillow I was out like a light. Next thing I knew, my alarm was waking me up."

Abby's phone buzzed. She ignored it. "You keep an alarm while on vacation?"

"This isn't a vacation, remember? It's a paid gig." He took a sip of his tea and let out a satisfied sigh. "Speaking of which, do you have any leads on how to handle Violet?"

Abby leaned back, shaking her head. "I need to talk to her first. See if I can figure out why she's doing this and what's keeping her here."

Abby's phone buzzed again.

"Are you going to get that?"

"It's probably my mom."

"Or Mina."

Abby hid her frown behind her glass. Lucas was right, it could be Mina. As much as Abby enjoyed texting with Mina, she couldn't shake the feeling her dreams had left her with—that by flirting with Mina, she was hurting Chelsea.

Lucas reached for Abby's phone.

Abby tried to stop him, but by the time she set down her glass, he already had her phone in his hands.

"It's Mina." Lucas flipped the phone over and slid it back toward Abby.

The lock screen showed three missed texts from Mina, the contents of those messages hidden, waiting for her to unlock her screen.

Abby waved her hand. "I'll check them later when my fingers aren't covered in syrup."

Lucas frowned. "Are you two okay?"

"Yeah. Why wouldn't we be?"

"She hung up on you last night and now you're avoiding her texts."

Abby sighed. "I'm not *avoiding* her. I like her, okay? I like talking to her. I just…sometimes I feel like she wants more from me and I'm not sure I'm ready, you know?"

"More as in, responding to her texts?"

Abby made a face. "As in spending Valentine's Day together. Going on romantic dinners. She wants to take me to a fancy fondue restaurant—that's like *serious* date stuff."

"So tell her you want to go somewhere else."

Abby swirled her fork through her melting whipped cream. "I want to go. It's just the thought of a whole weekend where the two of us do nothing but romantic couple-y things is kind of terrifying."

"Why?"

"You know why."

"No, I don't. I would love to spend a weekend with Wanda, just the two of us, no distractions." Lucas adjusted his glasses and eyed Abby expectantly. When several seconds passed with faint jazz music filling the silence between them, he asked, "Is this about…someone else?"

"No," Abby said, stabbing her waffle. She knew he meant Chelsea, and appreciated that he hadn't mentioned her name. But she also hated that he had picked up on that. Sharing breakfast with him like this reminded her of all the Friday night sleepovers she had at his place. Instead of observing Shabbat, they would stay up late playing video games. Lucas would always sleep in, but his sister and parents were kind to Abby as they cooked an assortment of breakfast foods that filled the kitchen with delicious scents. And then Lucas would stumble downstairs in his pajamas, half-asleep, glasses askew, hair disheveled, and he would drag Abby out onto the back porch, where they could have some privacy to continue whatever conversation had kept them up that night—usually something minor like their latest theories on a TV show or webcomic, but sometimes they would talk about the big stuff.

Like Chelsea.

But Lucas would always wait for Abby to bring her up.

Abby sighed. "Maybe. I don't know. One minute, I'm with Mina and things are great and I'm into her and we have a nice moment—and suddenly I get all panicky, like by being with Mina I'm somehow hurting Chelsea."

Lucas nodded like Abby's tangled thoughts somehow made sense. "You're not hurting Chelsea."

"I know." Abby touched a pale patch of skin on her left wrist, where—until recently—Chelsea's bracelet had lived for nearly a decade. She tried to put into words the complicated tangle of emotions that stemmed from her desire for Mina because, the happier she was with Mina, the more guilt she felt that this happiness came from Chelsea's absence. "But what if her spirit is still out there? What if I just haven't found her yet?"

Lucas rubbed his chin, a thoughtful expression knotting his brow. After several long seconds, he shrugged. "What if she is? What if you go back home and she's waiting on your doorstep?"

Abby's heart lurched with hope at the thought, despite its impossibility. "You know that's not how it works."

"I'm just saying—if Chelsea is still out there and you find her—maybe soon, maybe years from now—don't you think she would want to see you happy?"

Abby rubbed her thumb across her glass of orange juice, leaving a syrupy thumbprint behind. "Well, yeah. But I just imagined doing this kind of stuff with her, you know? So when it happens with someone else…"

"It feels unfair?"

"It's complicated."

Lucas nodded. "Have you talked to your therapist about this?"

Abby shook her head. She hadn't talked to her therapist in over two years, but Lucas didn't need to know that. It wasn't like she *needed* a therapist. She had been doing well. No grief-stricken episodes or flashbacks. And she doubted her therapist would believe her experiences with ghosts.

"Dating again is big. I think this is something you should talk to her about."

"Fine. I'll call her when I get home. But for now, can we please just focus on getting rid of this ghost? What did *you* learn about Violet?"

Lucas looked like he wanted to say more, then shook his head and slipped his phone from his back pocket. "Not much. She died in 1975 in a kitchen fire, as Sam said. She'd been working at the bed and breakfast for about nine months before that—ever since graduating from the local high school. She was an only child, buried in a small cemetery, a few miles from here."

Abby chewed her lip. "Where did she live?"

"In Hartford. About a thirty-minute drive. But she was staying in the bed and breakfast to be closer to her boyfriend."

Abby felt a pang of longing and sadness as she realized Violet's life bore a striking resemblance to Chelsea's. Had she had plans to meet her boyfriend after work that night, just as Chelsea had planned to meet her? She cleared her throat. Violet hadn't died in a car accident. She had burned to death, surrounded by people who could have saved her. And yet, she sacrificed herself for them. Or so the story goes. "We're sure the fire was an accident? No one suspected foul play?"

Lucas shook his head. "Not on record, anyway."

"Did anyone benefit from her death?" Abby thought aloud. "Did they inherit a lot of money? Did her parents disapprove of her boyfriend? Did she have some secret that her employer didn't want to get out?"

Lucas gave her an incredulous look. "How am I supposed to find that out?"

"With your internet searching."

"That's not public information."

"But she's dead. And her family is probably dead. Doesn't that make it history and therefore in the public's best interest?"

He adjusted his glasses. "That's not how it works."

Abby finished chewing a large bit of her waffle before responding. "Well, see what you can find out about her family and her employer—anyone who may have had a motive to kill her."

"You really think she was murdered?"

"I have no idea," Abby confessed. "But it seems like something we should rule out before we confront her."

Lucas rubbed his chin. "I'll head to the library and see what I can find. In the meantime, do you want to try talking to her again?"

"Later," Abby said. "First, we have a ghost tour."

"ARE YOU SURE this is a ghost tour?" Lucas whispered, shuffling against the carriage's velvet seat as Abby scrambled in beside him.

"Yeah." Abby tucked her short windswept hair behind her ears. "Why do you ask?"

Lucas gestured at the flowers covering the heart-shaped hood. "It seems kind of romantic."

"Well yeah, it's Valentine's Day. The Valentine's Day tour is in season. But Jeffery here said he'd give us the ghost tour instead, right, Jeffery?"

"I did," said an old man, who stroked each white horse before climbing up to the driver's seat. "It's the same route, different stories. Although instead of the pub where the ghost tour usually ends, I'll be dropping you off at the Spring Meadow Inn for the chocolate festival."

Lucas—who had looked as if he was preparing to jump out of the carriage—sat back down at the word 'chocolate.' "Is that festival free?"

"With one of my tours, it is."

"Sweet!" Lucas beamed, snuggling back into his seat. "Isn't Spring Meadow Inn the rival inn Sam's on about?"

"There are only two hotels of note in the area," Jeffery said, even though Abby was pretty sure the question had been directed at her. "Spring Meadow if you want something modern, and Willow's Edge if you want something quaint. If you ask me, they're less rivals and more what you're in the mood for. Alright, lovebirds—sorry." He cleared his throat and continued in a lower, somber tone, "Alright, soon-to-be departed souls. Hold on to your seats as we dare to venture through this town's sinister past."

Lucas gulped. "This dude just got creepy."

"Think of the chocolate," Abby whispered back, tucking

her hands into the sleeves of her oversized flannel.

"Our journey begins with the body entombed in the church on Strawberry Meadow Drive…"

The carriage's steady bounce paired with Jeffery's voice lulled Abby into a cozy sleepy state, as she followed his tales of ancient deaths and suspicious disappearances. She and Lucas traded whispered jokes about their guide's theatrics, until they approached the bed and breakfast. The tone quickly grew serious.

"Over one hundred years old, this charming bed and breakfast is home to a tragic resident. She's often called the Star-Crossed Waitress, but we locals call her the Girl in the Red Dress."

"Violet Lovelace," Abby said automatically.

"Why yes." Jeffery nodded his cap in Abby's direction. "She is most frequently seen wandering the back garden in a red serving dress. Violet was a waitress, serving a dinner party in 1975, when the kitchen caught fire. In the chaos, they say her final words were to her lover, asking him to meet her behind the building, but she never made it out. She waits for him to this day."

"This just got scary," Lucas hissed.

Abby ignored him. "What else do you know about her?"

Jeffery shook his head, pulling the horses to a stop at a red light. "Not much, I'm afraid. She was on that TV show, the one where a crew stays the night and tries to prove the place is haunted. They said they heard her calling out to her lover. There's also a bit about her in the book *Haunted Connecticut: Tales from the Beyond*. I can get you a copy if you'd like."

"I bet you could," Lucas muttered. "This guy would sell anything."

"How long have you been doing these tours?" Abby asked.

Jeffery straightened, leading the horses into a steady gait once more. Their hooves clattered on the asphalt as the carriage rolled forward under a tunnel of evergreens. "About seven years now. Of course, this is the first ghost tour I've done in February."

"Have the stories about the bed and breakfast changed at all?"

Jeffery shook his head. "Not really. And before you ask, no, I haven't seen the ghost. But I've got enough people who've told me similar stories, I believe them. And there's weird stuff that's been happening in that place, especially in the last few months. I blame it on the show—it aired last December. Ever since then, there have been guests leaving in the middle of the night, staff quitting left and right. If you'd asked me a few weeks ago, I'd have said the owners were trying a little *too hard* to play up the haunted house routine."

"You mean you think they staged it." Abby recalled Sam's pride at reigniting interest in Willow's Edge Bed and Breakfast and wondered for the first time how far they would go for publicity—surely not to the point of shoving someone down the stairs.

"It crossed my mind. Got them a fair amount of attention around Halloween. But now—their reviews are dropping, staff is turning over—doesn't make sense."

The wind picked up, sending Abby's hair over her eyes. She retucked it behind her ears. "In your genuine opinion, do you think it's haunted?"

Jeffery shrugged. "Could be."

Abby waited for him to say more. When he didn't, she

prompted, "Have you heard of any other ghosts in the house?"

"The Wentworths are mentioned in a few places. Charles Wentworth was the original owner of the place. His son, John, turned it into a bed and breakfast. They were a kind family. They say you can see them occasionally from an upstairs window."

"What about Matilda?" Abby asked.

"Who?"

"Matilda Burke, Charles Wentworth's granddaughter."

"You sure know your history. I haven't heard of her," Jeffery admitted. "You want to take the next part of this tour, or should I?"

"Carry on." Abby settled back against the velvet seat of the carriage as the horses carried them forward, around a small bend toward a haunted bookshop. She half listened to the tale of a ghost cat who haunted the second-floor balcony as her mind wandered to Chelsea. Somewhere out there, was a tour guide speaking of Chelsea's death? Surely not—a car accident is too brutal and too common a death. Ghost tours play off drama and the morbid fascination of a rare death, decades or centuries old, so the listener can feel safe and secure thinking that won't happen to them. It's quite awful, really, to think about how some deaths become tantalizing tales or tragic warnings while others fade out of existence, forgotten entirely.

"Oooh, I see chocolate!" Lucas clapped his hands as they approached a brick building with a small table out front between large cardboard cutouts shaped like chocolate hearts. A couple approached the table, gloved fingers entwined, as they took a pair of pink tickets. "That's what I'm talking about!"

The carriage pulled to a stop in front of the table. Jeffery dismounted and opened the door beside Abby. "Your haunted drinks—uh, indulgent chocolate—await."

"Thank you," Abby said, handing Jeffery a tip. "I've always wanted to go on a haunted tour."

"Might I suggest going at night next time?" He offered Abby his hand, but she was already jumping down. "In October. It's much more atmospheric that time of year."

"If you go at night, you're going alone." Lucas scrambled out of the carriage, loosening his scarf. "The daytime was bad enough. Night would be terrifying."

"If you decide you want the proper Valentine's Day tour, I'll give you fifty percent off." Jeffery waved as he climbed back into the driver's seat. "We also offer Christmas and historical tours. Same deal."

Abby waved goodbye, before turning her attention to the woman collecting tickets for the chocolate festival. She handed them each a raffle ticket, map, and goodie bag filled with chocolates before ushering them through a pair of double doors to a room filled with booths advertising everything from chocolate-covered strawberries to chocolate sculptures.

Lucas's jaw dropped. "I think I've died and gone to Heaven."

Abby grinned. "I thought you'd like this part."

"We could have just bought tickets here, though. That tour guide was creepy and we didn't learn anything."

"We learned something," Abby countered. "These hauntings are recent. They started around Christmas. Let's see if something changed around then."

Chapter Five

After several hours at the chocolate festival, Abby and Lucas returned to the bed and breakfast with sugar-fueled energy and a basket full of chocolates.

Wind hummed through the pines, scattering dried needles around their shoes. A cardinal soared overhead, chirping past a freshly painted wooden sign that advertised the 100th anniversary of the first Valentine's Day dinner. A paint can rested beside it, brush on top.

"Should we write our initials?" Abby teased.

"Don't you dare." Lucas guided Abby further from the sign.

"I was only joking."

Lucas shook his head and then nodded toward the wicker basket in her hands. "I call dibs on those butterscotch toffees."

"You can't call dibs on my prize."

"I thought you said you'd share."

"If you share the fancy massage you won."

"You can't share a massage."

"It's a couple's massage."

"Right. And we aren't a couple." The breeze picked up, sending frosted pine needles swirling across the steps. They crunched under Lucas's sneakers as he climbed to the front porch. "I'm going to call and change it to a solo massage."

Abby slipped a brass key from her pocket and fiddled with the lock on the front door. "Why don't you just change it to a best friends' massage?"

Lucas resumed shaking his head. Behind him, Harvey stood on a step ladder, wrapping red garlands around the columns on the front porch, his uniform splattered with red paint. He glowered at Abby and Lucas as if their presence annoyed him.

Abby waved. "Love the sign!"

He grunted in response.

Abby pulled open the door and stepped into the lobby. Warmth settled over her, relaxing her muscles as the scent of freshly baked bread filled the air. "A man of few words. I like it."

Lucas shut the door behind him. "I don't think he likes us."

"I don't think he likes anyone," Sam added, straightening a vase of roses on the front desk while Cupid circled them with a bone. "How's the ghost hunting going?"

"Good," said Abby, although she wished they had learned more by now. "I can confirm the house is haunted."

Sam's attention sharpened. Glancing over their shoulder, they guided everyone into the back office, securing the door after Abby, Lucas, and Cupid entered. They closed the blinds and turned to Abby. "Violet?"

Abby nodded. "She's here."

"Not right now," Lucas clarified, assessing the room with the binoculars. "Abby saw her in the back garden last night."

"And there are two more ghosts," Abby explained, taking

in the cramped space with mismatched office furniture. Two desks faced each other with a narrow walkway between them. Bookshelves lined the far wall, broken only by a portrait of a dark-haired white man taken some time ago. One desk had a large desktop computer and tons of small gothic trinkets, including rock skulls, miniature Halloween figurines, and creepy dolls. The other had a framed wedding photograph of a middle-aged man who looked nothing like Harvey and a blonde woman who looked nothing like Susan; several neatly stacked documents, and a pen holder.

Sam sank into a chair behind the cluttered desk. Cupid dropped his bone at their feet and Sam halfheartedly tossed it across the room. The dog scuttered after it, his claws scratching against the hardwood floor. "Any idea who these other ghosts are?"

Abby cleared her throat. "Charles Wentworth and Matilda Burke."

Sam tapped their chin. "Matilda…Matilda. I don't think I've heard anything about a Matilda living here before."

"She's Charles Wentworth's granddaughter."

Sam shook their head. "We don't have any record of her."

Abby nodded. "Charles Wentworth told us."

"And the internet confirmed it," Lucas added, holding up his phone.

"I wonder why she wasn't mentioned in the *History of Willow's Edge*?" Sam mused, borrowing Lucas's phone to scan the page. "That's the book we have to read during onboarding."

"Is Violet in the book?"

"Yeah. It's here if you want it," Sam picked a thin paperback book off the shelf and handed it to Abby. It was more of a pamphlet, thirty pages at most, but nicely bound with a glossy cover.

Abby handed it to Lucas. "See if there's anything we can learn about Violet and what could be keeping her here. Is there anything that changed around Christmas? Did you sell—or advertise selling—something that could be meaningful to her?"

Sam shook their head. "No. And I'd know if anything changed. There hasn't been anything beyond routine maintenance."

"What's routine maintenance?" Abby asked.

Sam shrugged. "Replacing lightbulbs, cleaning supplies, the occasional broken dish or lamp."

"Do you have any of her personal belongings?"

Sam scratched their head. "I don't think so. But we've got a lot of antiques around here."

"The article I found said everything was returned to the family," Lucas explained.

"Maybe she really is waiting for her boyfriend to return," Abby theorized with a pang of sadness. Could Chelsea still be roaming the parking lot, waiting for Abby to meet her at the movie theater? Abby made a mental note to check when she got back home. "What happened to him?"

Abby and Sam looked at Lucas expectantly.

Sighing, Lucas slipped his messenger bag off his shoulder and removed his laptop. "I'll see what I can find."

Abby began to pace, Cupid trailing her, while Lucas's fingers clicked across the keyboard. If the boyfriend still alive, he might have some idea of what happened to Violet's belongings—and what could be keeping her here. If he wasn't, well—maybe they could reunite their ghosts. Reuniting a vengeful ghost with their remaining family had worked last time. If Violet's unfinished business is waiting for her boyfriend, that could work. And on a deeper level, she couldn't deny the fact that if someone found Chelsea's ghost, she would want to know.

A loud crash came from outside. Cupid ran to the window, barking intently, his tail flicking the curtain.

Sam jumped, slamming their knee into the desk. They let out a string of curses.

Lucas dropped to the floor, covering his head with his hands. "What was that?"

Abby rushed toward the window. Lucas reached for her arm as if to stop her, but she brushed past, gently nudging Cupid aside so she could pull open the curtains. The dog shrank behind her, whining.

Sunlight rushed into the cramped room. She had to blink a few times for her eyes to adjust. Rocking chairs swayed gently in a ruby glimmer coming from the freshly hung garlands. Nothing suspicious caught her attention.

"Where's Harvey?" Sam asked.

Abby's gaze darted to where the ladder had been moments before. It was no longer in sight. The garland he had been hanging spiraled halfway up the column, then trailed loose as if he had run out of tape.

She cracked open the window and leaned her head out, ignoring the icy chill. "Harvey?"

A muffled sound came from across the front lawn. For a moment, Abby feared he had fallen, but then he stepped into view and she saw him running toward the house, hand over his mouth.

His gaze met Abby's and he stopped short. Fear flickered across his face. He grabbed hold of the porch to steady himself.

"Hold on, we're coming!" Abby shouted, pulling the office door open and hurrying onto the porch. "What happened?"

"We heard the crash," Sam added, rushing to Abby's side. "Are you alright?"

Harvey looked from Sam to Abby, eyes wide and alert. "You didn't see?"

"Didn't see what?" Abby asked.

Harvey shook his head and pointed a trembling finger toward the front walkway, where a trail of paint-splattered footprints led from his boots to the freshly painted sign. "See for yourself."

Abby's stomach churned with apprehension as she started across the lawn. Brittle grass crunched under her sneakers. The chilling breeze teased the hair on the back of her neck. Soon she stood before the sign advertising the Valentine's Day dinner. Well, it *had* advertised the Valentine's Day dinner. The word 'Valentine's' was now crossed out, a new word glistening over the top: *Remembrance.*

Remembrance Day.

Sam's jewelry clanked as they moved beside Abby. A soft gasp slipped from their lips.

"What is it?" Lucas called from the front porch.

"Vandalism," Sam said briskly. "How did this happen?"

Harvey hobbled down the stairs, shaking his head. "I don't know. I was letting the first coat dry and I went to hang the garlands on the front porch like you'd asked. I didn't see anyone, besides these two."

He pointed an accusatory thumb at Lucas and Abby.

"We didn't touch it," Lucas insisted.

Sam nodded in acknowledgment.

"They weren't here long enough to do anything," Harvey

confirmed. "But a few minutes later, I heard a sound. Like wind rushing through the trees. But I didn't see anyone. Then a bush rattled and I started walking around, thinking maybe some kids snuck in here playing hide and seek or something. That's when I saw it."

"The ghost?" Lucas speculated.

"The sign. Startled me so much, I stumbled back and tripped over the damn paint can." He gestured toward a bed of rocks where an overturned can oozed red paint into the grass.

Sam hurried to return the can to its upright position. "We need another camera for the front porch. If anyone steps foot on this property, I want to know."

"Cameras won't help unless they pick up ghosts," Harvey muttered.

"And we need to clean this up. Nathan's flying in tonight. If he sees this, he'll freak."

Harvey let out a loud, weary sigh and moved toward the front door. "I'll get some rags."

"I'll help." Abby jogged to catch up with him. He was old enough; he must have been alive in the seventies. Maybe he knew something about the night that Violet died. "So you believe in ghosts?"

Harvey grunted, wiping his shoes on the mat before stepping inside. "I believe we should let the dead rest in peace."

"Are you from around here?" Abby followed him to a small closet cramped with cleaning supplies. She had to step over Cupid's bed to reach it, and even then most of the supplies were on a shelf too high for her to reach.

Harvey handed her a stack of rags. "What's it to you?"

"Were you here the night of the fire? Did you know the girl who died?"

"Violet?" Harvey let out a weary sigh. "Yeah, I knew her. The whole town did. It was a real tragedy. Something you don't forget, you know? I wasn't at the party, but I was in town. It was a horrible night."

He shook himself, turned, and locked the closet door. "Like I said, the ghosts are better left to themselves."

Abby followed his gaze to Violet's photograph over the display of ghost books. "You think Violet's ghost was disturbed somehow?"

Harvey shrugged, rubbing the base of his shoulder as if it pained him. "All I know is that these hauntings started not long after they announced bringing back that damn dinner party. It doesn't seem too hard to put two and two together."

Her sneakers squeaked across the polished floor as she followed him back to the front door. "You're thinking the talk of the party woke her up out of some kind of slumber or something?"

"I don't know. You're the ghost expert. You tell me."

"It could be." She needed to pay Violet another visit. It was time to find out what exactly she wanted.

Chapter Six

Abby sat on the swing for two hours waiting for Violet, but she never appeared. After finishing a third episode of her favorite podcast, she searched the grounds with no luck. Violet was nowhere to be found.

"She's not around much," Charles offered from his rocking chair on the second-floor landing. "Only a certain time of day."

"Evenings?" Abby asked, trying to recall precisely what time she had seen Violet the previous evening.

Charles kept his expression bland. "If you want answers, you know what you need to do."

Abby remembered his request for the croquet rackets and resolved to ask Sam if they could set up a game in the evening.

"There you are," Lucas said, walking down from the top floor in a dark burgundy uniform complete with a tasseled cap. The designers were probably going for a bellhop, but he looked more like a toy soldier. "Where's your uniform? Have you cleaned a single room yet?"

Abby sighed, shaking her head. "Not yet. Have you?"

"I have. Check-in starts in thirty minutes. We've got three new guests tonight, and two have special packages that we need to take to their rooms."

"You're treating this like a real job." Abby slowly climbed the stairs to the top floor.

"Because it is a real job."

"For like three days." Abby slipped her uniform off the hanger. She removed her binoculars and sweater, then pulled the jacket over her T-shirt.

Lucas had his back turned to give her some privacy. "That's three days of pay that I could use. And Sam's job is on the line if we don't perform."

"Okay, okay." Abby removed her jeans next, replacing them with thick black trousers. They were a little loose, while the jacket was a little tight, but all things considered, it was warm and comfortable to move in. She placed the hat over her head, secured the strap below her chin, and clipped the walkie-talkie on her belt. The binoculars didn't quite fit in her pocket, so she hung them around her neck. "Ready."

Her stomach growled.

Lucas turned around and raised an eyebrow. "Did you eat lunch?"

"Not yet," Abby admitted.

He grabbed a granola bar from the kitchenette and tossed it to her.

Abby dodged, allowing it to fall to the bed behind her. "I've got a better idea."

"WE CAN'T JUST walk into the kitchen," Lucas protested, pointing at the sign that read 'Staff Only.'

Abby flicked the tassels on his hat. "We're staff, remember."

"But—"

Abby shoved open the double doors and stepped inside a warm rectangular kitchen that smelled deliciously of sweet bread and coffee. White cabinets lined the walls, broken by a few windows on the right side. It was surprisingly cozy for its size, with flour sprinkled across the counter, a heap of dishes in the sink, and various ingredients huddled across the kitchen island. Magnets with motivational quotes lined the doors to the large fridge and freezer, and a few delicate embroidered flowers hung from the occasional cabinet. Susan leaned against the back wall, scrolling her phone. She glanced up, waved half-heartedly, and returned to whatever video she was watching.

"Did you make these?" Abby asked, pointing to an embroidered rose.

Susan removed her headphones. "What?"

"Did you make these?" Abby repeated, tapping the embroidery as she stepped deeper into the kitchen. "And do you have anything good for lunch?"

Susan beamed. "I did. They're gorgeous, aren't they? Make the place feel like home. There are some granola bars in the pantry. Scones will be done in five minutes."

"Scones sound perfect." Abby leaned against the counter, relishing the scent of fresh bread.

"We don't have five minutes." Lucas tapped his watch. "Grab a granola bar and let's get going."

Sighing, Abby opened the pantry and marveled at the size. It was larger than any closet she had seen, almost the size of her apartment's kitchen. She stepped inside to survey the rows of snacks.

The granola bars were near the front, but Abby scanned the rest of her options. Several clear plastic storage boxes showcased various baked goods including banana bread, starberry jam cookies, and brownies. She pulled down the box of brownies and cracked the lid. An irresistible aroma of dark chocolate and sweet raspberries greeted her. She turned back to Susan to ask for a napkin, but Susan already had her headphones back in and was texting someone, with an annoyed expression. Abby picked up a decent-sized brownie and returned the box to the shelf. "Do we really have that much to do?"

"Yes. I took a bottle of wine and some chocolates to Sarah Jane. We need to take a cheese and charcuterie plate to John, but we can wait until they check in. Magnolia needs a delivery of roses, and Charles has the romantic setup of a century."

Abby found it difficult to focus on Lucas's words as the brownie was even more delicious—and gooey—than she had anticipated. "Meaning?"

Lucas handed her a napkin, then slipped a piece of paper from his pocket and read, "Champagne on one nightstand, chocolate-covered strawberries on the other. Roses in the vase by the TV. Arrange the box of rose petals in the shape of a heart on the bed. Place a box of bath supplies on the bathroom sink and a dozen LED candles around the room. Arrange the towels in the shape of a swan—"

"Jeez, these people go all out for Valentine's Day."

"I know, right?"

Abby finished her brownie in two extra-large bites and wiped her lips. "Guess we better get started. You know, if you put this amount of detail into solving our ghost case, we'd have our culprit by now."

"I *do* put this amount of detail into our case," Lucas countered, leading the way out of the kitchen. "After we finish these rooms, I want to look at those pictures of the messages again."

"You think they can tell us more about who left them?" Abby asked, careful to avoid Harvey, who was setting up the dining room tables for dinner.

"Maybe." Lucas quickened his steps to keep up. "I've been thinking about the sign we saw out front. It didn't have a curlicue."

"A curly cue?" Abby asked. "That sounds like something you'd order at a drive-through."

"It's an embellishment," Lucas explained. "The 'm' has this little curl in the top corner. Check the message drawn in lipstick, you'll see."

Abby slowed in the lobby and reached for her phone but stopped short as she noticed a woman in a purple leather jacket sitting in the waiting area, flipping through a *National Geographic* magazine. Dark wavy hair cascaded past her shoulders, one side tucked behind a triple-pierced ear. Her combat boots, painted with bright butterflies, rested on a drawstring gym bag.

Abby's heart fluttered. "Mina?"

Mina glanced up from her magazine, grinning. She jumped to her feet and started toward Abby, slowing a few steps away. Her smile still shone, but her expression suddenly became apprehensive. "Hey."

"What are you doing here?" Abby rushed forward, meeting Mina in a warm, comforting hug. Mina's familiar scent enveloped Abby as her arms wrapped around her shoulders, pulling her close.

"You invited me." Electric light gleamed off Mina's eyes, illuminating the shadows underneath. Abby wished she could brush away the bags as easily as she had brushed crumbs from her uniform. "Did you change your mind?"

"No, I'm glad you're here," Abby assured her, hugging her tighter before taking a step back. "I just didn't expect it. I thought you were working until Saturday."

"We wrapped early. I tried to tell you last night but—"

Abby wrinkled her nose as she recalled how she had left Mina on hold while she questioned Charles. "Sorry."

"I thought I'd surprise you." Mina shrugged, a hesitant smile twisting the corner of her lips. "Surprise."

Abby bit back a grin. "It's a really good surprise."

"But?"

Abby's heart fluttered as Mina's smile slipped. Abby longed to pull her close and kiss her wavering lips, but another part of her wondered *what comes next*? Mina was here, which meant she was expecting a *real* date. Maybe they would go to a romantic dinner and come back to watch movies by candlelight. Maybe they would go on a dozen dates, or a hundred—until one day Abby would be waiting at a restaurant or a park or a coffee shop and Mina wouldn't show up and she would hear sirens, or maybe the sound of a collision, and she would hear those dreaded words *there was an accident*—

Abby swallowed back her feelings, gesturing toward her uniform. "But I'm kind of in the middle of a rush—"

"She slacked off all morning," Lucas supplied.

"I did not *slack*. I was ghost hunting, which is what I actually took this job for."

"But we're getting paid to clean. And decorate." Lucas pointed to the vase of roses behind the concierge desk and then upstairs, reminding Abby they needed to bring it to one of the guest rooms.

Abby glanced at Mina's gym bag, resting on the floor near where she had been sitting. It was the only luggage in sight. She slipped her room key out of her back pocket and handed it to Mina. "You can put your things in the room."

"Which one?"

"Third floor," said Abby at the same time as Lucas said, "Fourth floor."

Abby frowned at him. "It's on the third floor to your right."

Mina raised an eyebrow. "You got separate rooms?"

"She took the haunted one."

"Ah." Mina smirked, flipping the gold key between her ringed fingers. "Sounds about right."

The fluttering in Abby's chest grew stronger as the urge to lean forward and kiss the curve of Mina's lips grew. She took a step back. "I'll meet you back here in an hour?"

With a mock salute, Mina picked up her gym bag and slung it over her shoulder, heading toward the stairs.

Abby picked up the heavy vase of roses with a sigh. "Let's get this over with."

Chapter Seven

Dim light flickered from the electric chandelier, spilling golden rays across the Charles room.

Lucas shuddered. "This room gives me the creeps."

Abby set her bouquet of roses on the mahogany nightstand and stepped back, surveying the dark wooden furniture and leather armchairs. Nearly everything was dark brown, red, or gold. "It looks like the Fire Nation designed it."

"I was thinking Dracula." Lucas drew back the burgundy curtains, letting a stream of sunlight brush the carpet as he eyed the dark wardrobe suspiciously. "Just in case."

Abby glanced at the bathroom, which was surprisingly larger and more luxurious than Violet's. With a garden tub, fountain shower, and marble countertops, it was the perfect spot to unwind. Abby longed to take a nice long bath and let the jacuzzi jets massage the stress right out of her. A large oval mirror hung over the single sink, sparkling against a golden frame. A familiar frame. Abby slipped her phone from her pocket and scrolled to the images Sam had sent of the previous messages, confirming her suspicions. "This is where one of the messages was written. *Join me.*"

"Focus, Abby." Lucas reminded her. "We won't discover anything if we get kicked out of here."

He had a point. With a sigh, Abby pocketed her phone, turned off the light, and left the bathroom.

It took three trips to get the welcome gifts into the Charles room, and nearly half an hour of watching YouTube videos to transform the towels into suitable resemblances of swans. When Abby had satisfactorily decorated the room with LED candles, she attempted to place the final one on top of the wardrobe but found she was too short to reach. She jumped and tossed the candle, which rolled to the side. The room shook as she landed.

Lucas winced. "Abby, I swear to God—"

"I couldn't reach!"

Shaking his head, Lucas abandoned the flower petals he had arranged in the shape of a heart on the bed and moved to Abby's side. As he retrieved the candle and returned it to an upright position, Abby slipped the binoculars out from under her uniform and peered through the window, searching for signs of Violet.

The front yard beckoned in a warm afternoon glow. Sun gleamed off the fountain, casting gold rays across the surrounding hedges. A stain from the spilled paint marred the grass, reminding Abby of the danger they were all in.

A soft *creak* drifted through the room.

Lucas backed away from the wardrobe. "What was that?"

"Probably someone walking upstairs."

"It came from the *wardrobe*," Lucas insisted. "Not upstairs."

"Then you must have bumped something in there." Lowering the binoculars, Abby stepped toward the wardrobe to prove her point.

Lucas grabbed her arm. "What if someone's in there?"

"No one's in there."

"You don't know that."

Abby suppressed an eye roll as she reached for the brass knob and opened the door to the wardrobe. Creaking, it revealed a dimly lit space, empty except for gently swaying hangers. "See? No Narnia kids."

Lucas frowned. "I could have sworn it came from in there."

"It must have come from the hall." Abby shrugged and turned toward the door. As soon as she opened it, Cupid dashed inside, a pale plastic bone in his mouth. He dropped it at Lucas's feet, bowing toward him with a playful bark.

Abby laughed. "It's just Cupid."

"Come on, boy, you shouldn't be in here." Lucas reached for Cupid's bone and tossed it into the hall.

Abby glanced at the clock. She had fifteen minutes before she needed to meet Mina. That was long enough to question Violet if she could find her.

"Where are you going?" Lucas asked as Abby was halfway out the door.

"I'll be right back," she called, hurrying upstairs.

Lucas sighed. "Somehow, I doubt that."

She barely heard the words. He probably meant to keep them to himself, but Abby had picked them up before the door swung shut behind her. They carried a strong hint of annoyance. She paused, turning back to the door, debating whether she should return and find out what was bothering him. She wanted to do this as a team, to remind Lucas how well they worked together; maybe then he would consider paranormal investigating as a real career move.

But she could lose her chance to talk to Violet.

Turning back to the stairs, she noticed the door to Magnolia hung open. A quick knock on the door and unanswered greeting confirmed it was unoccupied, though the sheets were rumpled, a small suitcase rested in the corner, and the nightstand was cluttered with a charger, paperback books, and a teacup stained with lipstick. She cut through the heart of the overwhelmingly pink room, straight to the window, bringing the binoculars to her eyes.

The swing remained empty, hovering in the shadows. Through the binoculars' warped lenses, the oak's pale branches gleamed like bones reaching toward the swing as if to pluck at something—or someone.

Stepping back from the window, she caught the edge of a dark-haired ghost standing beside her and yelped in alarm.

The binoculars fell to the floor with a crash.

Lucas ran in. "What is it? What did you break?"

"Nothing," Abby said, relief slowly seeping the fear from her veins as she remained warm, with no ghostly hands wrapped around her neck or objects flying in her direction. "I just saw a ghost."

Lucas's eyes narrowed in suspicion. "Isn't that your job?"

"She was right there, okay?" Abby held her hand inches from her face to demonstrate. Taking a deep steadying breath, she managed to turn on the walkie-talkie and raise the binoculars without trembling.

The curtains swayed ever so slightly in the heat rising from the radiator. Slowly, she moved her gaze from the window toward the loveseat.

The ghost stood behind it, leaning against the back as if she were waiting casually for Abby to invite her to sit and chat. She smiled, but there was nothing friendly about her smile. Her dark hair hung loose and tangled around a simple navy dress with a wide collar that jutted out in sharp angles around her pale neck in a way that reminded Abby of a cartoon villain. The worst of it, though, was the way her lips curled upward in a gloating manner while her pale eyes bore directly into Abby with such force she nearly dropped the binoculars again.

Abby hesitated, waiting for her to speak. It was clear she had been watching Abby for some time, and was finding amusement in Abby's fear. But the woman didn't speak, just continued her unsettling smile without breaking eye contact.

"How long have you been watching me?" Abby asked.

The woman straightened with a shrug and waved her hand gracefully through the air. "Not much. Just here and there, since you arrived."

"Is that Violet?" Lucas asked.

The woman laughed in a manner that could only be described as a cackle. The sound made the hair on the back of Abby's neck rise. "Of course you'd ask that. Why does it even surprise me anymore?"

"So, you're *not* Violet?" Lucas asked.

"No," she snapped, pacing dramatically from one end of the loveseat to the other, her dress flaring around her with every turn. If this woman auditioned for the Wicked Witch of the West, she would get the part. Assuming they hired ghosts. "Contrary to popular belief, she isn't here."

"You're Matilda," Abby deduced.

The ghost stopped, turning to Abby with wide eyes. "You've heard of me?"

"Charles told us about you."

"Wait a second." Lucas moved toward the suitcase and flipped over the luggage tag. "This is Dr. Greenwood's room."

"This is *my* room." The teacup rattled as Matilda rushed toward Lucas, glowering. Her hands turned into fists but remained clenched at her side as she turned back to Abby. "What are you doing snooping around *my* room?"

"Looking for—" Abby chewed her lip. She had been about to say 'Violet,' but decided that wasn't a good idea. "Ghosts."

Matilda's nostrils flared at the hesitation. "You mean *her*."

"Violet," Lucas confirmed, returning to Abby's side. Without the binoculars, he couldn't see Matilda's expression. He continued, oblivious to the fact Matilda rushed toward him for a second time, shaking her fists in his face. "We really should get going. If we're caught trespassing in Dr. Greenwood's room, my career is over."

"Well, she isn't here," Matilda spat. "And if she was, I wouldn't tell you."

She stormed to the opposite side of the room, disappearing through a bookshelf.

Abby lowered the binoculars to find Lucas blinking in confusion. "She seemed upset," he said.

"That's an understatement." Abby switched off the walkie-talkie and glanced at the digital clock on the nightstand. Its modern red glow slashed the antique furniture in harsh rays. Five minutes until she was supposed to meet Mina and she wasn't any closer to finding Violet.

"Oh my god," Lucas exclaimed, his voice hitching.

"What?" Abby raised the binoculars back to her eyes, checking for a ghost or hidden message.

Lucas knelt by the nightstand. "She's reading *Legendborn*."

Abby blinked, realizing that what she had mistaken for horror was instead excitement. "What's that?"

"Only one of my all-time *favorite* books. It's YA, so professors usually dismiss it, but Dr. Greenwood has taste." He pointed at the leather bookmark sticking out two-thirds of the way through. "Looks like she's almost finished."

That was Abby's cue to leave. She handed Lucas the binoculars and walkie-talkie. "Call me if you find anything that actually matters."

"This is your job, Abby. I'm not doing it without you."

"*Our* job," Abby corrected, heading toward the door. "I figured I'd take the night shift. Unless you'd rather swap?"

"Enjoy your dinner," Lucas called back, his tone instantly perkier. "I've got this covered until sunset."

The door clicked shut behind Abby. Her sneakers pattered softly against the carpet, stirring up bits of dust and dirt as she moved to the stairs. Someone should vacuum the landings. That *someone* was probably her. She added it to the mental list of things she had to do and didn't have time for. The list was growing by the minute.

Shoving down all thoughts of cleaning and investigation, she descended the stairs.

Mina waited for her in the lobby, as magnificent as ever. Her dark hair was freshly swept to one side, her makeup refreshed, and her former travel clothes had been replaced with a surprisingly fashionable sweater. Not that Abby knew much about fashion, but Mina always seemed to go for practicality over style. Aside from her bridesmaid dress, this sweater was the fanciest thing Abby had seen on her.

It looked good. Flattering. *New.*

Like she was trying to impress Abby. The thought brought warmth to Abby's heart while simultaneously fueling the nerves in her stomach.

"Hey." Abby tried to keep the nerves from her voice. "You look nice."

"You look like you're still working."

Realizing she was still wearing her work clothes, Abby groaned. "One sec."

She hurried to the office and flung it open. Thankfully, it was unoccupied, so she didn't have to explain herself as she slipped off her hat and jacket, tossing them on the back of the chair. Snatching a pen from Sam's desk, she searched for a piece of paper. The leather-bound notebook looked too fancy to rip a piece of paper out of and the only stack of stationery she found were gold-lined thank-you cards.

She considered texting Sam, but it occurred to her that Harvey or Susan might come in, see the discarded clothes, and think she had quit—or worse, that something bad had happened to her.

She then noticed a piece of paper in the trash can. It lay crumpled in the bottom of the clear liner, wedged between a chewing gum wrapper and an empty package of candy hearts.

It looked big enough, and clean enough, to write on.

Abby picked up the wadded paper and flattened it out. On one side was a handwritten letter that she had no intention of reading, but the calligraphy caught her attention. Each of the 'm's had a fancy swirl in the upper left corner. A curlicue.

Her innocent act of scrawling a note quickly turned to snooping. She couldn't help herself. She was curious.

Dear Sam,

It has come to my attention that you have granted a team of paranormal investigators free rein to the bed and breakfast. While I have no problem with this per se, please remember to reach out to me prior to any future publicity stunts. Any articles, blog posts, books, or film media these paranormal investigators want to publish will need to go through our standard press approval process. Make sure they don't write anything that contradicts the brand we have worked so hard to build—warm, welcoming, historical, and, yes, a bit haunted, in a harmless, entertaining way.

I'm concerned these rumors of guests and staff leaving in the middle of the night are too much. We want to allure guests, not frighten them.

See if these paranormal investigators can post something before the Valentine's Day dinner. Maybe we can get the local news involved, stir up interest for next year. Would be great if we could get Violet to appear (ha)!

Sincerely,

Nathan

Abby read the letter twice, before setting down her pen and running her hands along the edges of the paper. This Nathan guy sounded like he didn't believe in ghosts, but he was willing to spread rumors for good marketing. And he seemed to think Sam, as head of his marketing team, would go along with his plan.

She thought back to when she first talked to Sam about the investigation. Sam had asked for her services in ridding the place of the ghost. They'd mentioned nothing about publicity. For the first time since her arrival, Abby wondered if her cousin was actually open to believing in ghosts, or if they had an ulterior motive in inviting her here.

She scrunched the paper into a tight ball and tossed it back where it belonged. It slammed against the wire trash can before falling listlessly to the bottom.

One thing had become clear—it would be impossible to make it through dinner without thinking about work.

Chapter Eight

Abby managed to keep her attention on Mina the entire walk to the casual pizza place two blocks down, during the short wait for a table, and while the hostess seated them in a cozy two-person booth. Then she launched into a recount of the letter she had just discovered.

Mina's eyes narrowed. "You think Sam's pretending the bed and breakfast is haunted to stir up publicity?"

"No," Abby insisted, fidgeting with the corner of a laminated menu. "It *is* haunted. Sam knows it. Or I'm pretty sure they do. But this Nathan guy seems to think it's all made up."

"So what?" Mina leaned back in the booth across from her. "Why does his opinion matter?"

His opinion didn't matter, but Sam's did. While Abby and Sam hadn't been particularly close in recent years, Sam had always treated Abby with respect and had taken her at face value. They never once questioned Abby's complicated feelings around Chelsea's death, never criticized her career choices. Back when Abby started high school and shared her dreams of moving to LA to become a movie star, Sam was the first person who encouraged her. They had taught her about mood boards and passed along news of auditions. The thought that her cool weird cousin who believed in the impossible could doubt her ability to communicate with ghosts—or, even worse, could trick her into using them for a publicity stunt—was deeply unsettling. Before Abby could articulate this, a waiter stopped by to take their order (two sodas, no straws, and a cheese pizza to split). As he walked away, Mina drummed her fingers on the table, looking thoughtful.

Elaborate shades of blues and purples coated her fingernails, reminding Abby of the night sky. As she studied them, she noticed the occasional tiny ghost peeking out from the dark.

"Do you like them?" Mina asked, following Abby's gaze. "I thought about painting them your favorite color, but I realized I don't know what it is."

"I don't have one," Abby admitted, her cheeks warming at the thought that Mina had painted her nails *for* her. "I love all the colors."

Mina laughed. "Of course you do."

"They look amazing." Abby reached across the table, taking Mina's hand for a closer look. Her long, graceful fingers were warm and soft, and Abby wanted to savor their comforting feeling as long as possible. "Did you paint them yourself?"

Mina nodded. "It's been a while since I've done anything this intricate. I have to remove them for work, so I guess I got out of the habit."

Every detail was perfectly executed. Unlike Chelsea, whose bold artistic brushstrokes covered every space she occupied and every outfit she wore, Mina kept her artistic side close, small, but equally magnificent. It must have taken her hours to paint such intricate designs, and so few people would even notice. When Abby finally managed to pull her eyes away from the miniature art galleries on the tips of Mina's fingers, Mina was grinning at her.

"What?" Abby asked.

Mina shook her head, giving Abby's fingers a gentle squeeze before taking her hand back. "Nothing. I just forgot how cute you were in person."

Abby felt the blush creep up her cheeks. She dropped her hands to her lap. "I would say the same, but it's hard to forget how hot you are."

Mina's lips curved up, her eyes shining with amusement. "Does that mean you still want to date me?"

"Of course. That's why we're here, isn't it?"

The grin slipped down Mina's lips, barely hanging on as she gave a stiff nod. Was there hesitance there? Abby couldn't be sure. Mina *had* said this was a date, right?

Yes, otherwise Abby wouldn't have been so worked up about it. She must not be doing a good enough job of making it *feel* like a date.

"I'll stop talking about work," Abby said quickly, trying to bring the smile back. "The rest of the night, it's just the two of us, promise."

"It's okay." Mina's shoulders relaxed and the smile revived itself. She reached for a rolled set of silverware in a jar at the end of the table. "I like how invested you get in things. At least your job is interesting."

Abby nodded. Interesting was one word for it. Complicated was another. "I just don't get why Sam would tell their boss that I was fake. Or that this was all for some Marketing stunt.

They wouldn't say that. There must have been some sort of miscommunication."

"Have you asked them?"

"I haven't had a chance."

"You can call them now if you want."

Abby considered it, then shook her head. If she called, it would come across as accusatorial. She needed time to think of the right way to approach the subject. And, right now, she wanted to focus on Mina. "It can wait."

The warmth in Mina's expression solidified Abby's choice. She tilted her head, her studded earrings sparkling in the fluorescent lights. "And how are you holding up with all of this?"

"What do you mean?"

"I mean, being back in a haunted house, surrounded by ghosts."

Abby shrugged. "It's kind of my job."

"That doesn't mean you won't feel things."

Abby's stomach knotted as she recalled her dreams of Chelsea and the guilty feeling she had woken up with. Sharing that she still had complicated feelings for her late girlfriend would *definitely* ruin the moment. "I get scared sometimes. But not as much as Lucas."

An elderly waiter delivered their drinks and, shortly after, their pizza. Abby supposed the meal was delicious but she could hardly remember because she had been so focused on steering the conversation into something more lighthearted and—once Mina had gotten on board—laughing at Mina's hilarious recounting of pranks played on set.

As they left the diner, Mina extended her hand. Abby's slid into hers so easily, she barely registered what she was doing until their fingers were already intertwined. Mina's palm pressed firmly against hers, as warm and reassuring as her presence. Abby found herself grinning, leaning closer with each step until their arms were practically entwined as well.

Streetlight glistened off Mina's jacket, illuminating wisps of snow that fluttered sporadically to the sidewalk. Dusk bathed trees and houses in hues of deep blue, almost the exact shade as Mina's nails. Jeffery's carriage rolled past, faint jazz music seeping from the front as he pointed out historic landmarks in an overly wistful tone.

Mina's eyes sparkled with the reflection of string lights. "This reminds me of a place my mom took me once. Some small town in Virginia, I forget the name of it. She took me there for their Christmas Festival. We didn't even celebrate Christmas, but she saw how much I loved our neighbors' Christmas trees, so she took me to see them light a big one—it must have been twenty feet tall, at least."

"That sounds wonderful," said Abby, who also appreciated Christmas trees although her mother would never allow one in the house. Some of her favorite memories were of helping Lucas and his family decorate theirs. "Your mom sounds like she was a great mom."

"She was." Mina's breath released fog that hung in the air. She pulled Abby closer to her. "I wish you could have met her."

"Me too." Abby found herself feeling a genuine ache of loss for the woman she had never met. Had never seen a picture of. She imagined she looked like Mina, with more wrinkles and graying hair. She desperately wanted to meet this person who no longer existed.

Mina wiped the corners of her eyes—whether they were tearing up or she was protecting them from the cold, Abby couldn't tell. But when she turned back to Abby, she was smiling. "I loved that festival. I haven't thought about it in so long. We went ice skating and I got to try my first funnel cake."

"You ice skate?" Abby asked, trying to picture Mina on skates. It wasn't difficult considering her athletic physique—the challenge was imagining her in a dainty ice-skating costume. It was easier to imagine a wrestler in a tutu.

"Terribly," Mina said with a hint of humor. "I never took lessons or anything. I just enjoy running really fast with knives on my feet."

"When you put it that way, you sound terrifying," Abby replied. She had been grinning for so long, her cheeks were starting to hurt.

Mina laughed and the sound brought life to Abby's already frantic heart. For the third time that day, she felt the urge to pull Mina toward her and press her lips against Mina's wide grin. Abby settled by tightening her grip around Mina's hand and leading her up the front steps of the bed and breakfast, feeling safer and happier than she had in a long time.

That changed when she stepped inside and saw Sam charging down the stairs, a frightened expression on their face.

"Abby, thank god!" Sam cried in relief. "We have an emergency."

Chapter Nine

Abby stiffened, breaking away from Mina as worry flooded her previously joyous thoughts. "What's wrong? Where's Lucas?"

Sam took a series of deep breaths, before pointing upward. "Charles."

Abby was already rushing upstairs. At first, she thought Sam had meant Charles had hurt Lucas, but then she realized Sam had pointed at the Charles room. The wooden door hung open, spilling light onto the burgundy carpet.

"Lucas!" Abby called, her cry echoing off the walls. She never should have left him. The number one rule of ghost hunting was to never split up. At least, that should be a rule. She would make it a rule, when she got around to the paperwork.

As Abby reached the second-floor landing, Lucas peeked his head around the corner, filling Abby with a sense of relief. Still wearing his uniform, he looked as unharmed and put together as ever.

"Shh!" He brought a finger to his lips and whispered loudly, "People could be sleeping."

Abby's hand flew to her heart. "I thought something horrible had happened."

"It did," Lucas said, inching the door wider open.

As the familiar gothic room came into view, Abby realized at once what was wrong. All their hard work from earlier—the carefully arranged towels and petals—had been destroyed. Petals lay scattered and wrinkled all over the floor, towels strewn haphazardly in the corners. Only the LED candles remained in some form of arrangement, but they were not where Abby and Lucas had left them.

They now stood in the middle of the floor, flickering around a row of candy hearts.

"What happened?" Abby asked. "Did Cupid—"

Lucas shook his head, ushering Abby deeper into the room. "Check the hearts."

Abby took a tentative step forward and crouched at the edge of the candles. The hearts lay face up, their messages smeared off, except for a single letter per heart.

M-U-R-D-E-R-E-R

"Well, that's concerning." Mina's voice served as a calming presence. Her hand went to Abby's shoulder, sending a jolt of warmth through her.

"Did you see who did this?" Abby asked, rising slowly to her feet.

Lucas shook his head and resumed sweeping petals into a dustbin. "I checked with the binoculars—whoever did it was gone by the time we found it."

"Who is 'we'?" Abby asked.

"Sam found it like this," Lucas amended. "They called me,

frantic, asking if we knew anything. I said we didn't. That it had been great when we left. And that we locked it." He lowered his voice to a whisper. "We did lock it, right?"

Abby's brow wrinkled. She couldn't remember. Lucas wouldn't have left it unlocked, though. He *always* locked up. At least, at home he did. And a locked door wouldn't deter a ghost anyway. "Did the camera get anything?"

Lucas arched an eyebrow. "You think the ghost will show up on camera?"

"Worth a shot."

"I'll ask Sam to check later. We've got important guests coming any second, so this needs to be picked up ASAP."

Abby reached for a towel and attempted to fold it back into a swan, before giving up and folding it like a normal towel. "You found it exactly like this?"

"More or less." Lucas dumped the roses into the trash. Too many were torn, smashed, or dusty to go back on the bed. Hopefully, they would be satisfied with the champagne and fruit, which were thankfully untouched. "We've cleaned a bit. Don't worry, I took pictures first. I'll show you when we're done here. And we didn't touch the hearts or candles."

As Lucas mentioned the candles, Mina picked one up. "Where do these go?"

"Anywhere less sinister," Lucas said.

"They were around the edges of the room," Abby added, reaching for a candy heart. She picked up the green 'M' and held it to the light. She rubbed her finger slowly across the faded letters. It was faintly damp as if the ghost had rubbed a damp cloth over the letters it wanted to smear. Strange. She pocketed it, then gathered the others.

"We don't have time to decorate." Sam returned with a

fresh bouquet of roses that they placed on the nightstand. Abby recognized it as the one from Violet that the previous guests had left behind. "Leave the candles, just shape them into a heart or something."

Abby moved to Mina's side and helped her arrange the roses.

The doorbell chimed.

Sam instantly straightened, their face draining of color. "That's them!"

"What do we do?" Lucas asked.

"Finish this and get out of here," Sam replied, hurrying to the stairs. "I'll stall as long as I can."

Abby's fingers flew around the LED candles, gliding them across the carpet until they resembled a shaky but passable heart.

Lucas tied the trash bag and slung it over his shoulder, which—paired with his red uniform—reminded Abby of Santa Claus.

The room wasn't quite as romantic as before, but it looked less like a horror set and more like a cozy hotel room, so it would have to do. Abby set a final candle on the nightstand and joined her friends in the hall.

The stairs creaked, as several pairs of feet ascended from the first floor.

"Your room is right this way," Sam said a little too loud and eagerly. "You must take a moment to observe these portraits. This here is of Charles Wentworth. He was the first person born in this house, in 1863, just three years after the home was finished. The detail is immaculate. If you look close, you can even see the gold embroidery on his jacket."

"Would you look at that!" said a male voice, lifting in awe.

"You really can."

Sam peered around the corner, giving Abby a desperate glance.

Abby nodded, confirming that the room was good to go. She let out a sigh of relief, rounding the corner.

A loud crash echoed through the landing.

Lucas stood, mouth agape, the trash bag open at his feet, spilling rose petals onto the hall floor.

Abby turned to see what had scared him, fearing some message they had missed. The far wall glistened in the light of electric candles, as spotless as ever. Each door remained shut, the decor in place.

Sam stood on the landing, matching carry-on suitcases in each hand. The guests behind Sam stopped in their tracks, staring at Lucas.

In the split second before Lucas spoke their names, she understood.

The important guests that they had spent so much time preparing for were not strangers at all.

Chapter Ten

"**M**ichelle?" Lucas's voice hitched, his jaw locking into place. "What are you doing here?"

"I could ask you the same thing." Michelle folded her arms across her lavender sweater. From her French manicure to her tight bun, she was as prim and polished as ever.

Sam glanced between her and Lucas with wide eyes. "You two know each other?"

"Yeah," Lucas grumbled.

At the same time, Michelle snapped, "I'd recognize my little brother anywhere."

Sam made a rather humorous attempt to hide their surprise. It didn't work.

Michelle stepped closer to Lucas, looking him up and down. "Are you *working* here?"

"Temporarily."

"I thought you just got an apartment back in Virginia?"

"I did."

"But you took a job in Connecticut—" Her eyes narrowed, jumping to Abby. "With Abby?"

"Temporarily," Lucas repeated, tugging on the edge of the trash bag.

Michelle rounded on her husband. "Did you know about this?"

David shook his head and stepped forward, trying to defuse the situation. "What a pleasant surprise."

Michelle stepped past David, leaning so close to Lucas she could have headbutted him. Instead, she shoved a finger against his chest. "What are you doing here? No lies, no games."

Lucas backed away, his shoe catching on the edge of the trash bag, spilling more petals across the burgundy carpet.

Michelle's eyes widened. "Are you stealing?"

Abby started to protest, but Mina put a hand on her shoulder.

"It's nothing like that," Mina said. "He and Abby are investigating."

Michelle's shoulders relaxed the slightest bit as she turned to her friend. "Investigating what?"

Mina gave her a knowing look, then pointed to the binoculars around Lucas's neck.

Michelle threw her hand to her forehead and groaned. "Ghosts?"

"We'll stay out of your way," Lucas assured her.

Electric light bounced off Michelle's amethyst earrings, scattering across the carpet. She rubbed between her eyebrows. "You swear you had no idea we were coming?"

Lucas shook his head.

"We had no idea," Abby confirmed, nodding toward Sam, who ducked sheepishly behind a pole, clearly not wanting to be associated with Abby at the moment. "My cousin hired us."

"When you say hired, you mean to clean, or—"

"To investigate the ghosts," Abby said, receiving a look of disapproval from both Sam and Michelle.

"Why don't we talk more in the morning?" David said diplomatically. "It's late. Let's all get a good night's sleep and we can talk more over breakfast."

"Great idea," Abby said.

Shooting Abby an annoyed glance, Lucas cleared his throat. "We won't be joining you for breakfast. We aren't guests."

"You aren't staying here?" Michelle asked, looking relieved.

"We're staying here, but in more of a faculty capacity," Lucas explained awkwardly.

Raising an eyebrow, Michelle surmised, "So, your breakfast isn't included and you want us to pay for it?"

Lucas shook his head. "That's not—"

"If you're offering, that would be wonderful," Abby said.

Michelle's lips narrowed into a fine line.

"It would be our pleasure," David said in a manner that sounded so *sincere* and oblivious to the brewing tension, she almost wondered if he hadn't been listening to the conversation. Or maybe he was just that nice of a person. Or maybe he had so much to spare, paying for three extra breakfasts really was no trouble at all.

It was probably a combination of the three.

With a charming grin, he moved past the others toward the Charles room. "It's this one, right?"

It took Sam several seconds and twice as many blinks to realize that they were being addressed. Slinking out from around the corner, they straightened their uniform and nodded curtly. "Yes, that's right. The luggage rack is in the coat closet to your left. If you need anything, please give us a call with the bedside phone, by pressing one."

"Thank you," David said with so much enthusiasm even Michelle's spirits seemed to warm. She smiled at Mina, waving fondly as she followed David inside, and shut the door behind them.

Sam leaned against the wall with a heavy sigh, looking as if their knees might buckle out from under them.

"That went well," said Abby.

Sam, Mina, and Lucas gave her incredulous looks.

She shrugged them off. "We got everything ready and made it out in time. David and Michelle were so surprised to see us, they won't notice if their towels aren't perfect swans, or if their roses are the wrong color—I doubt David even read what he ordered. He probably just picks the most expensive package at any hotel and leaves it at that."

The heat cranked up, creating a loud rumbling sound that echoed through the halls, sending frail warmth into the hall that only made the draft feel more pronounced.

Sam looked thoughtful. "Actually, the package was included with a gift card. They may not even know it came with the room."

Lucas's frown deepened. "But what if that ghost goes after my sister?"

Abby rubbed her sneakers against the carpet, gathering the fallen rose petals into a pile between her feet. "Better than a stranger. At least she knows what to look out for and how to protect herself."

Lucas unfolded his arms to pick up the fallen trash bag, carefully, with a hand on either side of the tear to minimize spillage. A few rose petals fluttered free. "But she's my sister,"

Lucas countered, sounding like a stubborn child.

"Then we better figure out how to send this ghost on," Abby replied.

"I've got this." Sam gestured to the mess between Abby and Lucas. "I'll finish cleaning up here before I head home for the night. Do whatever it is you need to, but don't bother the guests. That includes your sister."

"Got it," Lucas grumbled, handing over the bag and storming up the stairs.

Sam shook their head. "I can't believe he's related to the Kensingtons. Why didn't you tell me?"

"Why didn't you tell us your special late check-in was David and Michelle?" Abby countered.

"How was I supposed to know you knew them?"

"How were we supposed to know they were staying here?"

"It does seem oddly coincidental that we're all here the same weekend," Mina mused, returning a handful of crushed rose petals to the trash bag.

Abby nodded. She had been thinking the same thing, along with a sinking suspicion of an explanation. "You said they used a gift card?"

Sam nodded. "For the first night and the newlywed romance package."

"Any chance you can find out who gave them this gift card?"

Sam chewed their thumbnail thoughtfully. "I don't think so. Why?"

"I have a suspicion." Abby turned toward the stairs. She started to slip her phone from her pocket, then shook her head. It didn't matter why David and Michelle were there. They were a distraction—unwelcomed and unnecessary.

She needed to focus on finding whoever was leaving scary messages and cryptic threats.

She threw open the door to Violet, hurried to the writing desk, and took out a notepad. Her thoughts raced as she picked up a pen and proceeded to scribble them down in the shape of a bubble map.

"Why do I get the feeling that a cozy movie is not on our list for tonight?" Mina asked.

Abby stopped writing long enough to glance up and notice Mina sitting on the bed, leaning against the pillows, with a glass of wine in one hand. A stab of guilt cut through Abby, making her flinch. "I forgot about that."

Mina took a long gulp of wine. "I noticed. But you're working. I shouldn't have come without telling you."

"No, it's fine." Abby set her pen down and hurried to Mina's side, kicking off her sneakers as she flopped onto the thick duvet. "You're the best surprise. This can wait."

Amusement flickered across Mina's eyes. She sunk deeper into the pillows, setting her glass on the nightstand. "Somehow, I doubt that."

Abby leaped from the bed. "I just need a few minutes to check the security cameras."

Mina raised an eyebrow. "For what? A ghost?"

Abby shrugged. "One thing that's been bothering me about the mess we found in the Charles room is the candles."

Mina frowned. "What about them?"

"When Lucas and I decorated the room, there were a dozen, I'm sure of it. I distinctly remember putting one on each nightstand, one on the dresser, one on the wardrobe, three on the mantle, and five around the tub. It's possible I could have miscounted one or two candles but—"

"There were way more than twelve candles just now," Mina finished her line of thinking. Her brow furrowed as she no doubt recalled the sinister message inside the circle of flickering LED lights. Abby was definitely picturing it.

"Yeah. At least two dozen, maybe more. Which makes me think—how did a ghost get them up there? Sure, they can interact with the living, but we've only seen it in small ways and each interaction takes a toll on the spirit. How could a single ghost carry a box of candy hearts upstairs, erase their messages, bring a dozen extra candles, arrange them all, and turn each light on?"

Mina reached for her wine, shaking her head. "Until a few weeks ago, I never imagined a ghost could strangle someone either."

Abby ran her thumb over her neck, not wanting to think about the cold, invisible fingers that had held lace tight around that spot, nearly killing her. If this really was the work of Violet's ghost, she was *really* strong. Much stronger than anyone at the Kensingtons' home had been. "We need to see the security footage."

"Okay," Mina said. "But first, I want to give you something."

Mina reached into her pocket and pulled out a small bundle of tissue paper wrapped with string. She held it toward Abby expectantly. "Your Valentine's Day gift."

Abby felt her face grow warm while her heart beat faster. "I didn't know we were exchanging gifts."

"We aren't." Mina waved her hand. "I just wanted you to have this. I was going to give it to you under more romantic circumstances, but it may come in handy—hell, just open it and you'll see what I mean."

Abby took the small package carefully. It was surprisingly light. If Mina hadn't been so flustered, Abby would have thought this was a practical joke. But as she slipped the string off and the tissue fell apart, she saw something round and sunset-colored attached to a simple cord.

"It's a Himalayan salt necklace," Mina explained. "I thought it might help—you know, against the ghosts."

Abby delicately raised the cord, letting the pendant dangle over her extended palm. It sparkled faintly in the overhead light. She draped it over her head, letting it fall gently around her neck, the pendant resting inches above her heart. "It's perfect."

Mina drained her glass, stood, and stretched. "Let's check out that security footage before the ghost has a chance to erase it."

Chapter Eleven

"**P**lay it again," Abby whispered. She was so close to Mina that Mina's dark velvety hair fluttered against her sweater as she leaned forward. She savored the sweet nutty aroma she had come to associate with Mina's nearness.

Gray light spilled from the computer, illuminating a sliver of the office. With the blinds shut and darkness pressing in from all sides, Abby felt a bit like when she was a small child staying up late to finish a scary movie. Just like back then, she kept glancing at the door, fearing it would open despite the lock. Now, instead of fearing her mother would walk in, she feared someone more sinister would interrupt.

Mina tapped her ringed index finger against the desk and sighed. "I think three times is enough. There's nothing there."

But at Abby's request, she rewound the footage and skipped to the motion-activated clips again. In the few seconds she, then Lucas, emerged from the room, she was able to see the clean floor, the original bouquet beside the bed.

The door remained shut until Sam opened it at 17:47, and found the room in a disastrous state. From the camera angle, only half of Sam's face was in view, but the shock and horror were clear.

They must have shouted or made some sound of alarm that wasn't captured on the recording because Lucas came running. Abby watched herself and Mina walk on-screen moments later, and the blur of movement as they began to clean up.

"No one went in or out of that room between the time you set it up and when Sam found it trashed," Mina voiced in conclusion, even though Abby wasn't entirely ready to believe it. "The door didn't even open."

"But there must be *something*," Abby insisted. "Ghosts may be able to go through walls, but candy and candles can't."

"Even if a ghost is carrying them?"

"I don't think so," Abby admitted, wishing she had a way to test it out. She had certainly never seen it before, but then again, she still had a lot to learn about the paranormal. "They would at least show up on camera, right?"

Mina twisted a dragon-shaped ring around her thumb. "Maybe they were already there, under a sink or something?"

"Maybe," Abby agreed. She still felt like she was missing something.

She grabbed her coat. "I need to talk to Violet."

ABBY WAS RELIEVED to find Violet sitting on the swing, her pale blonde hair swaying gently in a nonexistent breeze.

She approached her cautiously, bundled in her jacket

and scarf, wincing as the cold night air grazed her cheeks. Small motion-activated lights flashed on and off as she and Mina moved through the garden, following their steps like a searchlight.

Faint romantic music drifted from the patio, where two elderly couples sat in the glow of flickering heat lamps, enjoying sweet-smelling desserts.

The music faded the further Abby moved into the garden. The light appeared dim and fractured through the binoculars. Abby stumbled on the uneven stone path, relieved when Mina's firm hands steadied her.

If Violet was frightened, she had more than enough time to run. But she remained on the bench swing, blinking curiously at Abby. Her soft voice crackled through the walkie-talkie. "You came back."

"I did," Abby said gently. "I get the feeling you want to talk?"

The ghost nodded, a resigned expression crossing her features. "Sure. It's been a while since I've talked to anyone. I forgot how nice it can be."

Wanting to tread lightly, Abby began, "Why don't you tell me about yourself?"

A sad smile touched Violet's lips. "I'm not sure I remember much. My name is Violet. I'm waiting for someone. My boyfriend." She touched the ghost of a ring on her finger. "My fiancé."

Fiancé? She said the word with such assurance, Abby was inclined to believe her. But Lucas hadn't found any news of a fiancé. "You're engaged?"

"Yes," Violet repeated, brightly, holding up her finger. Through the binoculars, the faint lines of the engagement ring formed a more solid band, as if Violet's memory created it: a simple diamond ring on an antique gold band. "He was supposed to meet me here. But…"

"But?" Abby prompted, taking in the new information. If Violet was engaged, why hadn't the papers mentioned it? Perhaps it had been a recent engagement—or recent breakup.

Violet shrugged. "I died."

Her expression hardened. She began kicking the earth, the heels of her Mary Janes stirring up the slightest cloud of dust. The swing rocked under her, chains creaking loudly over the distant music.

Abby heard Mina's sharp intake of breath behind her, surprised by either the pronouncement of death or the jolting swing.

Abby pulled her sleeves over her knuckles. At least Violet knew she was dead and she didn't have to deliver that shocking news. "Do you remember how?"

"A fire," Violet said sadly. "I don't remember the details. Just the fear and the heat—and then a sense of calm and peace that I can't really describe. Bliss, maybe? But a peaceful kind."

Abby exchanged glances with Mina. If Violet was telling the truth, she was far too at peace to be accusing someone of murdering her. "Do you know how long ago that was?"

Violet shook her head. She looked Abby up and down. "Months? Maybe years. The uniforms haven't changed much, but the guests wear different clothes."

"About fifty years," Abby said.

Violet let out a whistle. "I could have been a grandmother by now."

She kicked harder. The swing flew so close to Abby, she took a cautious step back. That peace sure had evaporated quickly. This was definitely a spirit that could have been leaving those messages. Perhaps even without remembering that she had done so.

"Tell me about your fiancé," Abby encouraged, hoping to steer the conversation back to something less upsetting. The breeze picked up, carrying a trace of smoke from a nearby chimney. "How long have you been engaged?"

"Officially, only a few days." Violet tucked her feet under her until she was sitting cross-legged. The swing continued swaying, though it gradually lost its vigor. "Unofficially, we've been talking about it for months. He's a great guy, you know. But my parents don't think so."

Abby wondered if perhaps he wasn't so great, and they had overlooked a key suspect in Violet's death. Perhaps the fiancé had been left out of the papers because he did something to hurt her. "Why don't your parents like him?"

"He doesn't come from money," Violet said with a shrug.

Abby felt her theory evaporating.

"But he's going to make it big, I know it," Violet continued dreamily. "He's great at baseball. Star player. Well, he was. Until he hurt his shoulder."

"What's his name?" Abby asked kindly.

"Harry. Harry Lardes. I bet he's a major star player. Or he *was*. I suppose he's retired now." She rested an elbow on the arm of the bench, sighing deeply. "Of all the places I could have ended up, this isn't the worst."

Abby supposed that was true, but she also pitied her. She couldn't imagine staying in one place for a year, let alone a lifetime. Maybe it was good that ghosts didn't have a clear understanding of the passage of time. Violet already seemed more at peace than she had mere moments ago. But if she had left those messages—even if she didn't remember doing so—then part of her clearly believed she was murdered. And that was the part that Abby needed to talk to. Abby braced herself. "I don't want to upset you, but I have to ask—is there any chance what happened to you was…not an accident?"

Violet blinked. "What do you mean?"

"Do you think someone started that fire intentionally?"

Violet shook her head. "No. I saw it happen. At least, I think I did. There was an oil fire. The new girl didn't know what to do, so she dumped water on it, which only made it worse. I ran to help her, but by the time I got there, I couldn't contain it. I told her to run, and I tried to go after her, but it was too late."

"I'm sorry," Abby said with genuine sympathy.

Violet shrugged. "It wasn't your fault, and like I said, I've been at peace."

Abby studied the calm, smooth lines of her face, the soft sparkle in her eyes. She seemed to genuinely believe her words. Which meant she *wasn't* the ghost behind those messages, but another dead end.

"Do you know what's keeping you here?" Mina asked gently, stepping closer to Abby. Abby relaxed at her proximity, her presence soothing.

Violet shook her head. "Wish I did, but I don't have a clue. There's nothing, pulling me, you know? No longing. I'm just… waiting. But I can't remember what I'm waiting for."

"Have you been in the house recently?" Mina asked, giving Abby an apologetic shrug for taking over the questions. Abby didn't mind. She liked seeing Mina interested and it was good to keep their list of suspects open.

She cautiously followed Violet's wistful gaze to the patio flickering with heat lamps and candlelight as the ghost answered softly, "No. Why?"

Her serene expression gave Abby the feeling that she was telling the truth.

"Did you know they're having another Valentine's Day dinner?" Mina asked.

"They have one every year, don't they?"

"Not since you died," Mina said flatly.

Violet's face fell. "How sad. It was groovy."

"It doesn't bother you that they are bringing it back?"

"Why would it? It has nothing to do with me. If I'd died on Christmas, I wouldn't expect the world to stop celebrating, would I?"

"I guess not," Abby agreed. She inched forward, pine needles snapping under her sneakers. "But someone is upset. Someone has been leaving angry messages. We thought that might have been you."

Violet blinked. "I haven't left any messages."

Abby lowered the binoculars to exchange glances with Mina, who was frowning.

"Who else could it have been?" Mina asked.

Abby paused to consider the question, then turned back to Violet. "Do you know the other ghosts? Charles and Matilda?"

"Mr. Charles is far out," Violet said with a faint smile. "When I first realized I was a ghost, he helped me understand what was happening. He used to visit me out here, and then he stopped. I saw him in the window one day after I hadn't seen him in a while, and I thought, why not pay him a visit? If he can come out here and see me, surely I can go in to see him."

"Could you?" Abby asked, genuinely curious.

A thin strand of hair that had come loose from her ponytail fluttered against her cheek. She tucked it behind her ear, looking forlornly at the house. "I got in easy enough, but there was a mean woman there. When she saw me, she was furious. She told me to get out. That it was her house, and I wasn't welcome. She was a spirit, like me. But she could *do* things. The first time, she just asked me to leave, but the second time, her eyes got all dark and she started making things swarm, like some kind of storm. I ran out, and I've never been back."

"What did she look like?" Abby asked.

"Like someone who didn't want to be bothered. Dark hair, fancy old-fashioned dress."

"That sounds like Matilda," Abby said, confirming her suspicions.

Violet shrugged. "I never stopped to get her name."

Abby nodded. Lowering the binoculars, she glanced at Mina. "Any more questions?"

Mina shook her head. "Not that I can think of. It definitely sounds like this Matilda woman is our messenger."

"That's what I was thinking," Abby admitted. She lifted the binoculars once more. "Thanks, Violet. If you see anything suspicious—like the mean woman causing more trouble—let me know, okay? We're staying in your room."

Violet frowned. "My room?"

"The Violet room," Abby explained, attempting to jog her memory. "On the third floor, backyard view."

Violet shook her head. "I never had a room here."

"Sure you did," Abby said. "For a few months, while you were working here."

Violet stood, folding her arms across her chest. "No, I didn't. I remember walking here each day. Sometimes Johnny—the owner—would take me home at night. I only lived a few blocks down."

"Well, it's that room." Abby pointed to the window. She

chewed her lip. If Violet had no attachment to the Violet room, then why did it have the most frequent hauntings? Did Matilda hate Violet so much, she was hoping some ghost hunters would come and vanquish her?

Violet nodded. "If I see anything, I'll let you know."

With that, she moved into the bushes and faded out of sight.

Abby lowered the binoculars and turned to Mina, who had already turned back toward the house.

"You know what would be nice right now," Mina whispered, sliding her gloved hand into Abby's. "A nice hot bath. I think the tub is big enough for both of us."

Abby's heart thrummed at the thought of her and Mina sharing such an intimate moment and what it might lead to. With a squeeze of her hand, she pulled Mina close. "That sounds amazing."

Mina's grin grew seductive as she kissed Abby's cheek. "I snuck a few rose petals. Figured they may come in handy."

Winking, she stepped back, pulling a fistful of rose petals from her jacket pocket.

The sight of them stirred up memories, first of the chaos in the Charles room, then from much longer back. One night, years ago, Chelsea had slipped a fistful of roses from her pocket, excitedly explaining how she had picked them up after her cousin's wedding and planned to incorporate them into an art piece. An art piece for Abby, which had never been delivered, but had debuted at Chelsea's funeral—finished or unfinished, no one would ever know.

Abby's stomach knotted. She pulled away from Mina, hurrying toward the back door.

"Let's save them for tomorrow. I'm exhausted. And I need to talk to Charles."

In the dark behind her, Mina let out an exasperated sigh.

Guilt added itself to the turmoil of emotions festering in Abby's stomach. She couldn't keep avoiding Mina. She didn't *want* to keep avoiding Mina. But she couldn't stand there and kiss her while Chelsea consumed her thoughts.

Tonight was not the night for romance. Abby's stupid past had made that clear.

Which meant tonight would be reserved for putting troublesome pasts—and spirits—to rest.

Chapter Twelve

Abby did not put any spirits to rest that night. She stayed up until midnight, searching for signs of ghosts, but none appeared. No sound came through the walkie-talkie, no messages manifested on any walls, windows, or mirrors—the place was suspiciously quiet.

Eventually, she climbed into bed beside Mina, who was already snoring, and turned off the light. She checked her phone, scrolling through the images of the previous messages. Lucas was right. The handwriting looked different. Not only did the curlicue appear on the 'm' in the message written in lipstick, but it was far more fluid and bubbly than the remaining messages. Even the question mark was drawn differently than the question mark in the first message.

Abby rubbed her chin. What did that mean? Were they written by different ghosts? Had Matilda been exchanging messages with someone else?

Abby tried to read them all in order, as if two people were

talking to one another:

> *Don't you know this place is a tomb?*
> **Don't Forget.**
> *Ready to Join Me?*
> **...To my grave.**
> *You sleep on my bones.*
> **Murderer**

She shook her head. It didn't make any sense. With a yawn, she set her phone on the nightstand and fell into a pleasant sleep.

WILLOW'S EDGE DIDN'T just provide breakfast, it provided an *experience*. Or so the brochures said. As Abby stepped into the dining room, she could confirm the accuracy of that statement.

Sunlight soared through large windows, brushing golden rays across lace tablecloths and delicate china. Pink floral centerpieces posed on each table, their buds lifted high like royalty showing off their crowns. Airy romantic music drifted through the speakers, making Abby feel like she had stepped into a scene from one of those fancy historic shows.

Except—instead of wearing fine gowns and sleek suits— guests wore sweatpants and sweaters, yawning over hot cups of coffee while they scrolled their phones or read the newspaper.

Michelle and David were the only ones fully dressed, in complementary cashmere sweaters, looking at each other bashfully, like the stars of a romance movie. Lucas sat beside them, digging into his eggs Benedict.

"Good morning," Abby said cheerfully, and she took the

empty seat between Lucas and Michelle. Even the chairs were exceptionally comfortable.

Mina slipped into the chair across from her, between David and Lucas. Abby wondered if Lucas had intended to separate them so he wouldn't feel like the third wheel, or if he had merely wanted to keep as much space between him and Michelle and David as possible, accidentally separating Abby and Mina. Either way, she felt a surprising sting of disappointment as Mina moved out of arm's reach and her calming presence was replaced with the simmering tension between Lucas and his sister.

David alone returned Abby's smile. "Good morning. This place is lovely, isn't it? I slept like a baby last night. And the coffee is delicious! You have to try it."

"I don't drink coffee," Lucas replied, even though David had addressed Abby. He surveyed the rest of the room like he was looking for something.

"How long are you staying?" Michelle asked, slicing through crispy bacon. Her knife screeched against her plate.

"Until we can rid this place of its meddlesome ghost," Abby answered.

"Plus a few days, right?" Mina added, raising her hand to get Harvey's attention.

Harvey returned her gesture by raising his index finger as he finished pouring coffee for the table beside them.

"Right," said Abby. "If we finish before Sunday. I have work on Monday. But I can always find someone to cover for me."

Lucas gave Abby an incredulous look. "You're my ride. Aren't you going to ask me if I'm free?"

"You work remotely," Abby pointed out.

"It doesn't mean I don't have plans."

Harvey approached their table, slipping a notebook out of his pocket. "What could I get for you?"

"Coffee," Mina said, immediately. "And I'll take the oatmeal."

Harvey nodded, scribbling down her order.

"Do you have Lucky Charms?" Abby asked, flipping her menu open for the first time.

Harvey blinked. "I'll have to check."

"Well, I'll take that or whatever cereal you have, as long as it doesn't have raisins." Abby handed Harvey the menu before turning back to Lucas and adding, "What plans do you have on Monday?"

"I never said I had plans," Lucas responded. "Harvey, do you by any chance know if Dr. Greenwood will be down for breakfast?"

Harvey wiped his hands on his apron, glancing over his shoulder. He hesitated, then said, "Don't know if I'm supposed to talk about the other guests, but since you all are kind of staff, I happen to know she will not be joining us for breakfast. She requested service in her room this morning."

Lucas looked crestfallen.

Harvey patted him in condolence before retreating to the kitchen.

Abby frowned. "You said you had plans, just now. I said we could go back on Monday and you said you had plans."

"No, I asked if you were going to *ask* about my plans before making decisions that involved me."

Abby sighed. "I'm asking *right now*. What are your plans?"

Lucas took a sip of tea, set his cup down, and leaned back. "I don't have any."

Abby stared at him, her annoyance simmering into

frustration. "Then why did you want me to ask?"

"Because it's polite. It's not polite to speak for people without asking them first."

"You're the one who isn't being polite," Michelle said, glaring at Lucas as Harvey returned, refilling her coffee.

Lucas shook his head. "This doesn't concern you."

Michelle looked as if she were about to say more, but Harvey spilled coffee down the side of the mug and she jumped to her feet, yelping in surprise.

"Sorry, sorry," Harvey said quickly, reaching for a napkin in a poor attempt to soak up the dark blisters forming on the lace tablecloth. "Are you alright?"

Michelle nodded, rubbing soothing circles with her hand against her neck. "Yes. It just startled me."

Harvey, clearly uncertain of how to proceed, rubbed his finger over the stain as if hoping for magical bleach powers to set in. When they didn't, he moved Michelle's napkin ring over the stain and resumed pouring coffee in silence.

"The faster we vanquish this ghost, the sooner we'll be out of here," Abby stressed, attempting to reel the conversation back to something manageable. She nodded toward Michelle. "It would help if we had access to your room."

"Why?" Michelle stiffened. Abby wasn't sure if her sudden alertness was caused by the implication that her room was haunted or the fact that Harvey passed behind her, stumbling with the coffee pot.

"Something happened in there yesterday," Abby said, cutting straight to the point. "Before you checked in, someone—or some*thing*—trashed the place. I want to know who and why."

Michelle's eyes widened. "And you didn't think to tell us this *before* we slept there?"

David placed his hand over hers. "We slept fine. No one bothered us. I can check under the bed tonight if you want."

The rest of the table gave him an incredulous look. David didn't seem to notice. He patted Michelle's hand with a reassuring smile.

"I heard noises," Michelle insisted. "Footsteps."

"The walls are thin," David replied. "Besides, ghosts don't make footsteps. My house was haunted for decades and I never heard a thing."

Michelle glanced at Abby, her forehead wrinkled in concern.

"He's right," Abby admitted. "They don't usually make footsteps."

David returned his attention to smearing jam on his croissant as Mina took a loud sip of her fresh coffee. He leaned toward her, grinning. "Delicious, isn't it?"

Mina replied with a louder, longer sip.

"Put a circle of salt around the bed and you'll be fine." Abby dropped three sugar cubes into her own cup, where the velvety coffee swallowed them whole. She then poured a thin layer of milk and brought it to her lips. It was too bitter. She reached for more sugar. "Or better yet, let us vanquish the ghost for you."

"Should we switch rooms?" Michelle glanced toward David, concerned.

"It won't help," Lucas said. "It's happened in a few now."

Michelle leaned back, folding her arms across her chest. "Then I don't see why you need a key to *our* room."

Abby sighed. Michelle had a point. They already had access to Violet, which had also been the source of two hauntings. But she couldn't let the candles go. She supposed she could get the master key from Sam, but without Michelle's permission, she doubted Lucas would go along with her plan. Even for her, it felt like spying on a friend.

"What are your plans for today?" Mina asked, glancing between Michelle and David.

David grinned and explained animatedly, "I thought we'd take a walk around town, maybe stop at the bakery, before heading to lunch. We have reservations for a picnic on a boat—doesn't that sound nice? And then we're visiting a winery, and heading to dinner."

Mina took a long sip of her coffee and exhaled loudly. "That sounds a lot nicer than hunting ghosts."

"You could come with us," Michelle offered. "At least until lunch."

Mina shot Abby a look she couldn't decipher. "If you don't mind, I think I might."

The silence that followed was filled with the soft clacking of silverware and the steady roar of a radiator. Though everyone's eyes were on their plates or drinks, Abby felt like they were waiting for her to speak, to respond to some unanswered question of Mina's, but for once Abby didn't know what she was supposed to be responding to.

She studied Mina's face. It was a blank slate, as if she were intentionally trying to shield her emotions from Abby. Her eyes were narrowed intently on her coffee, which usually signaled anger or frustration. Was Mina angry with her for hunting ghosts? She knew that was why Abby was here. Was Mina frustrated that Abby wasn't spending more time with her? Then why didn't she ask Abby for more attention? Abby thought back to earlier that morning when Mina had asked her what their plans for the day had been. When Abby had gone over the proposed agenda, Mina grunted in response. Abby had assumed that was the closest she would get to enthusiasm before Mina had had her coffee, but perhaps there was more to it than that.

Whatever Mina was feeling, Abby needed to figure it out quickly, or she might lose her. Her stomach lurched with dread at the thought.

"Whatever you want to do is fine," Abby said, trying to sound supportive. "We can handle the ghosts without you."

Mina's expression grew even more pinched, her grip tightening on her mug, signaling that she was not pleased with this response. She tried to hide her emotions with a shrug, but Abby had already seen it.

"But I'll miss you," Abby added quickly. "And you can join us when you get back. It's very helpful, having you around."

Abby winced at the sound of her own words. She sounded less like the supportive girlfriend that she had been going for and more like a therapist complimenting a patient. Not romantic in the least.

Mina chugged the rest of her coffee and stood, heading toward the kitchen.

"Where are you going?" Abby called after her.

Mina held up her empty mug. "To get more coffee."

Abby watched her shove open the door to the kitchen without a second thought. Susan sat on the counter, grinning as she texted away on her phone until she noticed the oatmeal boiling over beside her. Abby wanted to follow Mina and ask what she was thinking, while at the same time wanting to respect her space. She glanced at Lucas for help. He was usually good with these emotional things. But his attention was on pouring a fresh cup of tea from a delicate porcelain pot.

David pulled a book from his pocket—Abby recognized it

from the gift stand—and began flipping through it.

"Is this your ghost?" he asked, turning the page about Violet toward Abby.

Abby shrugged. "Probably not. Everyone is always focused on her. I'm starting to think that's the problem."

"Who, then?" David asked, his green eyes filled with eager curiosity.

"Matilda Burke," said Abby.

David began flipping through the book, his eyebrows pinched together in concentration.

"You won't find her in there. She was never technically an owner of the house, and her death wasn't noteworthy, so she isn't mentioned in any of the materials. She's here, though, and I think she's jealous of the attention Violet is getting."

"You think she's our culprit now?" Lucas asked.

Abby nodded. "Ninety percent certain."

Lucas dropped his fork. It clanked against his plate, causing nearby diners to wince and glance over. "You could have given me a heads-up. I stayed up until midnight researching Violet."

"I didn't ask you to do that."

"Yes, you did," Lucas insisted. "You said, 'We better figure out how to send Violet on ASAP.' In order to do that, we needed to figure out what's keeping her here, and in order to do that, I needed to do research."

"Did you find anything helpful on Matilda?" Abby asked.

"No, because I was researching *Violet*."

Mina returned then, slipping into her seat with an annoyed expression. "What did I miss?"

"Nothing," Abby said heatedly.

Harvey arrived with their food, and they ate in awkward silence, broken by David's delighted exclamations about some historic fact or another he had learned about the town.

They exchanged relief-filled goodbyes as they returned to the main lobby and headed separate ways.

As Lucas started up the stairs, Abby grabbed his arm.

"Wait."

He looked at her expectantly. She took a deep breath. "I'm sorry I forgot to tell you about Matilda. I've been distracted. I want to solve this case *with* you. I want it to be fun, like last time."

Lucas raised an eyebrow. "What part of last time was fun?"

"Spending time together. Playing arcade games and drinking hot chocolate."

"We could have done that without the ghost hunting," Lucas pointed out.

"Not if the ghost killed us first."

Lucas sighed. "Alright, I accept your apology. From now on, we're partners in this. Anything you learn that you think is relevant, you let me in on. And I'll do the same. I like to know what you're thinking."

"Okay," Abby agreed, swinging open the door to the office. "Right now, I'm thinking we use a master key to sneak into Charles while your sister is out and—"

Abby stopped speaking as she realized there was a stranger standing in the middle of the room. He was a middle-aged man, with dark, neatly combed hair speckled in gray. He wore a sophisticated three-piece suit with a silver crest of the bed and breakfast on the front, looking far more put together than Sam, Harvey, and Susan.

"Can I help you?" he asked.

At the same time, Abby asked, "Who are you?"

The man frowned. "If you don't know that, you shouldn't

be in this room."

The back door slammed open and Sam stepped inside, Cupid at their heels. They looked between Abby and the stranger and began muttering a string of nervous apologies. "Sorry, so sorry. This is Abby and Lucas, the ghost hunters."

"Ah," the man said, kneeling down to greet Cupid. The dog pawed at his shoulders enthusiastically. "That explains why they were talking about sneaking into the guests' rooms. As understandable as it is, we really shouldn't allow that. If we were caught aiding that kind of activity, the legal fees would be outstanding."

Abby frowned, trying to place this man who acted like he knew her despite never having met her, while Sam practically groveled at his feet. He bore a striking resemblance to the portrait hanging between the bookshelves. And was almost an exact match to the groom in the framed photograph on the desk across from Sam's. "You're Nathan Wentworth. The owner of this place."

"Yes," he said proudly, standing and straightening his tie. Abby noticed he no longer wore a wedding ring, but there was a faint tan line around his left ring finger. "It's been in my family for generations. How do you like it so far?"

"It's nice," Abby admitted.

Nathan smiled, revealing a row of perfectly straight, extremely white teeth. "Charming, right? I have to say, I prefer ghostly publicity to come in October, but with the Valentine's Day dinner coming up, I see the potential. What with the dead waitress and all. You think the town would have gotten over it by now, but they're fascinated. What was it you said, Sam? Half our tickets sold from a paranormal site?"

Sam blushed guiltily, before nodding. "I can show them out if you'd like."

"Nonsense!" Nathan waved a hand dismissively, turning back to Abby and Lucas. "I want you to blog about that waitress. Nothing too scary, just something that will make people want to come back next year. Have her appear in the woods, looking longingly at the deck—or better, on the balcony—during dinner."

"We aren't bloggers," Abby said, realizing this was the same Nathan who had sent Sam the letter she had found in the trash. She liked him even less in person.

"And we don't fake ghosts," Lucas added.

"I hear you, I hear you," Nathan said dismissively, glancing at his watch. "Well, whatever it is you do, run it by me or Sam before the public sees, okay? And try to entertain the guests, don't scare them. I've got to run. My room's ready?"

Sam nodded. "I'll take you there now."

"No need," said Nathan, pulling open the door. "I know—Ah, careful, Harvey!"

Harvey stood in the doorway, blinking awkwardly like he had just been caught eavesdropping—or, more likely, waiting outside too terrified to come in.

He took a small step back, head down.

"Remember you're staying in Magnolia this time!" Sam called after Nathan. "Your usual room was booked!"

Nathan made no indication he heard their words as he continued upstairs.

Sighing, Sam ushered Harvey into their office and shut the door behind them. "Sorry about that. He's kind of—"

"A jerk," Abby said.

Harvey grunted in approval.

"—going through a divorce," Sam finished. "He was supposed to get in last night, but his flight was delayed. He's usually much nicer."

"Accusing people of being frauds isn't very nice," Lucas pointed out.

Sam sighed. "It's my fault he thinks this is a marketing stunt."

"Is it?" Abby asked, trying to keep the weight of her question from her voice.

Sam shook their head, the chains of their skull earrings clanging softly. "No. I'll admit, I'm trying my best to spin it positively—that is my job, after all. But the attacks are real. And they need to stop. I'd rather let him think we hired someone that took the theatrics too far than tell him I think the place is really haunted—he wouldn't believe me, and I'd probably be fired in a heartbeat."

Abby nodded, her shoulders softening as a sense of relief washed over her. Sam hadn't been entirely honest with her, but at least Sam believed her.

"Was it your idea to use Violet's face for the Valentine's Day campaign?" Harvey asked, his voice gruff against the muffled music and clanking dishes that came from the dining room.

Sam's eyebrows pinched together. "After Halloween, we had to do something to keep the momentum going. The ghost stories brought in more guests than the place had seen in years. How was I supposed to know it would upset her spirit or whatever?"

"I think it upset another ghost," Abby said, scanning the room with her binoculars to make sure it was clear of ghosts before continuing in a whisper. "She hates Violet. Won't let her in the house. Seems upset by all the attention she's getting, especially when no one's ever heard of her."

"You've talked to her?" Harvey asked, eyes widening in bewilderment.

Abby nodded, patting the walkie-talkie on her belt. "I don't think she wants to hurt anyone, just get attention."

"Violet?" Harvey asked, his face paling.

Abby shook her head. "Matilda. She wants attention. She's jealous that Violet is so beloved, while she's all but forgotten."

"So what if we give her attention?" Lucas suggested, his eyes brightening as his face took on the intense expression that often meant he was sorting out his thoughts before speaking: a talent Abby admired, but failed to do herself. She thought better out loud. "We could pretend we're doing a story on her."

Abby nodded. "That might help."

Harvey turned away, shaking his head and muttering to himself as if he wanted nothing more to do with this conversation or the ghosts they spoke about.

"You can vanquish her?" Sam asked, lowering their voice to a whisper.

"In theory," Abby replied. "But we'd need to know what's keeping her here. In the meantime, we could make both Matilda and Nathan happy by writing up a story about her."

"Maybe that'll help us figure out what's keeping her here."

"Digging two graves with one shovel." Sam nodded in approval. "Thanks for staying on top of this. I've really got to get back to work."

Abby retreated into the hall. "We do too. Lucas, grab the salt gun. I have a feeling we're going to need it."

Chapter Thirteen

After they'd changed into their uniforms and ensured the salt gun was properly filled, Lucas pocketed extra salt packets while Abby opened a box of candy hearts.

"Those things don't have much salt," Lucas pointed out.

"I know, but they're delicious." Abby popped one into her mouth. Lucas shook his head, but he was reaching for the box to take a handful himself. She let him, before shoving open the hall door and starting down the creaking stairs.

Abby tried to keep her attention focused on the task at hand, but her thoughts kept drifting back to Mina. As much as she told herself it was good for Mina to get out and spend some time with Michelle while Abby could focus on wrapping up this haunting, she felt a twinge of guilt accompanied by fear. Had she hurt Mina's feelings? Was Mina growing impatient?

"Are we actually going to write a story on Matilda?" Lucas asked from behind her.

Abby shook her head, attempting to clear her thoughts of

Mina. The faster they calmed Matilda down, the faster she would get to talk to Mina again and set everything straight.

"Sure, if that's what it takes to get her to stop hurting people."

"I take it I'll be the one writing it?"

"If you're offering." Abby stopped outside of Magnolia and knocked on the door. "Between the two of us, you're the better writer, after all."

"I write fanfiction, not news—"

The door opened and a thin blonde woman with a flowy blouse and long beaded jewelry stepped out. For a second, Abby thought she was seeing a ghost with her own eyes, but she quickly realized the woman was merely wearing pale foundation and exceptionally red lipstick.

"Dr. Greenwood," Lucas stammered, stepping beside Abby as if this was some once-in-a-lifetime celebrity meet and greet. "H-Hi. I—"

"I will not be needing housekeeping." Dr. Greenwood placed a 'do not disturb' sign on her door before shutting it in their faces.

Abby raised her fist to knock again.

Lucas caught her arm, guiding her forcefully away.

"Hey," Abby protested. "We need that room."

"You heard Dr. Greenwood." He pointed at the sign and held a finger to his lips.

"Yeah, I heard her being rude. But she's clearly awake and we've already disturbed her, so once we tell her that we aren't here to clean her room—we just want to talk to the ghost that's haunting it—she'll let us in."

"Or she'll get us fired. Nathan said we aren't supposed to bother the guests."

"But—"

"We're going to have to find some other way to reach Matilda. Maybe we can get her to come out here for her interview?"

Abby chewed her lip. It was worth a shot. She turned on the walkie-talkie at her hip and raised the binoculars.

"Matilda! If you can hear me, we want to talk to you."

"No need to shout," Lucas whispered, pointing once again to the 'do not disturb' sign on the door to Magnolia.

Abby rolled her eyes and continued, lowering her voice only slightly—the ghost still needed to hear her through the walls, after all. "We want to include you in our story."

The hall remained unchanged through the binoculars, its walls flickering with various wallpapers of past decades and foggy outlines of previous furniture. A chill crept up Abby's spine.

Lucas inched closer to Abby. "Why do I feel like she's about to jump-scare us?"

"She does love a dramatic entrance." Abby took a step back as a portrait warped and Matilda's pale face replaced it, her eyes gleaming as her lips formed a thin line. She emerged from the wall slowly, as if trying to disturb Abby with her wispy disjointed body. If that was her point, it was working.

"Thank you for joining us," Abby said, trying to keep the fear from her voice. "We want to tell your story. Tell us a bit about yourself. You grew up here?"

"I did." Matilda, now fully emerged from the wall, resembled her human self as she paced the top of the stairs, her dark hair fanning out around her in a nonexistent breeze. "It was… tolerable. Quieter than it is now, more peaceful. I suppose I had a happy childhood, though I never thought much about it at the time. I wanted to leave this place and start a family of my own."

Abby gulped. Matilda had died so young, sealing her fate away in this place for far longer than a lifetime. She asked gently, "You were in love?"

"Yes." A faint smile drew up the corner of Matilda's lips.

"What was his name?" Abby asked softly.

Matilda's dark eyebrows tilted together. "Her name was Alice."

"I'm sorry," Abby said, mentally chastising herself for assuming Matilda's sexuality. Charles had said she'd been in love with a guy. He had clearly been wrong. "Why don't you tell us a bit about her? How did you two meet?"

Matilda's face hardened. The air grew colder, nearby sconces rattling against the walls. "I don't want to tell you how we met. I'll tell you how she broke my heart. We were going to run away together, build a life together. She promised me. But—"

Downstairs, a door slammed open. Two sets of footsteps rushed down the hall, one loud and clacking, the other soft and heavy.

"Wait! Susan, please, wait—" a crisp masculine voice called. Abby recognized it as Nathan's.

"Why? Why should I wait any longer? I should have left ages ago, but—"

Lucas pulled Abby down, so they crouched behind the banister. Matilda's voice crackled through the walkie-talkie and Abby turned it off, lowering the binoculars to give Lucas a quizzical look. While the conversation sounded tense, she hadn't felt like they had been eavesdropping until now. If

Susan wanted to storm out in the middle of her shift, she had every right to.

"It's taken more time, I'll admit," Nathan said in a tender, reassuring voice. "I'm sorry. But I promise—by this time, next week. It'll really be over. You won't have to cook another meal in this place. And…my offer still stands, if you want it."

Abby frowned. By this time next week, what will be over? The hauntings? The overworked staff? Nathan was planning something, and Abby was curious how it involved Susan.

"I need to think about it." Susan huffed, her clacking footsteps retreating back toward the dining room.

"Take your time," Nathan called after her. "You know where to find me."

Through the banisters, Abby watched Nathan pace the lobby twice before leaving through the front door. She stood, brushing bits of carpet from her knees, starting toward the stairs to question Susan.

Lucas grabbed her arm, pointing to the walkie-talkie at her hip.

Right, Matilda. The walkie-talkie crackled as Abby turned the volume back up. She shook her head, clearing her thoughts. "Where were we?"

"You clearly don't find my life as interesting as that waitress," Matilda said. "I've changed my mind. I won't be talking with you anymore."

"That wasn't even Violet," Lucas protested.

Abby winced as the hall table rattled, the lights flickering.

"Don't bother me again," Matilda's voice boomed through the walkie-talkie. The portrait Matilda had crawled through lurched sideways, then slowly slipped back into place, remaining slightly crooked. The lights steadied.

Abby raised her binoculars. Matilda was gone.

"What now?" Lucas asked, the salt gun clenched between his hands.

Several yards away, a rocking chair creaked.

Abby sighed. "Now, we play croquet."

Chapter Fourteen

Croquet turned out to be a surprisingly easy game, once they managed to get it set up. The hardest part was dragging all the balls and mallets out of the attic and down three flights of stairs. The playing part was easy. At least, it was easy for Abby.

Lucas kept missing his shots, growing more and more flustered as the ghost of Charles loomed over him, directing his shots. "This game is for old white people," he muttered, as Charles scolded him for nudging the ball with his foot.

"You have to admit, it's kind of fun."

Taking another shot, which rolled directly past the hoop he had been aiming for, Lucas sighed. "I'd rather finish my book."

"Talk about old white people activities." Abby teasingly elbowed him before heading off toward her ball, which was two hoops ahead of Lucas's.

"Contrary to popular belief, there are a lot of famous Black authors," Lucas called to her. "James Baldwin, Langston Hughes, Toni Morrison—"

"Alright, alright." Abby held her mallet up in a sign of surrender, watching the ball she had just struck roll toward the nearest hoop and directly through, coming to a stop on the other side. She grinned. "I amend my previous statement. Reading is an activity for *all* old people."

"There are very successful Young Adult and New Adult authors—"

"I believe you. Please don't list them. It's your turn."

Lucas sighed, stepping into position and rolling his shoulders. For someone who claimed not to care about croquet, he sure was taking this seriously. He practiced his swing. And practiced again.

Abby pinched the bridge of her nose. He was probably just jealous she was beating him. He had always had a bit of a competitive streak.

"You sure you haven't played this game before?" Charles's voice crackled through the walkie-talkie, startling Abby, who had been so focused on Lucas she had nearly forgotten his presence.

"Nope," Abby said. "First time."

"You have natural talent."

Abby thought it probably had more to do with how much free time she had spent playing mini-golf. She had loved it until a few years ago when she worked at her favorite course, and it quickly lost its appeal. Still, she took the compliment. "It's fun. I see why you like it."

Lucas finally took his shot. The ball rolled straight toward the hoop. It crashed into the edge and spun sideways.

Lucas muttered something under his breath. From his

pinched expression, Abby could only be certain it wasn't positive.

"Loosen up." Charles's voice grew louder, clearly directed at Lucas. "You almost had that one, but you're stiff as a nail. Your aim will be better if you relax."

"It's hard to relax when there's a dead guy critiquing me."

He had a point. With each passing minute, Charles was acting less like a casual spectator and more like a coach.

"What can you tell us about Matilda?" Abby asked, hitting the ball toward the fifth hoop. She intentionally pulled her swing, letting the ball roll short of its target.

"So close!" Charles cried. "You almost had it! Just a little more *oomph* next time, and you'll be spot on."

"Noted," Abby said, before repeating her question: "What can you tell us about Matilda?"

She slipped her binoculars out this time, so she could see his face when he answered. It didn't disappoint. There was a longing in his eyes as if he hated to be torn away from the thrilling croquet game even for a moment to think of something as inconsequential as Matilda. He kept his gaze on Lucas as he replied, "What do you want to know? She keeps to herself. Has a bit of a flair for dramatics. I take it you've seen her whole gothic—oh my!"

He broke into a string of cheers, clapping as Lucas's ball rolled through the second hoop. "Well done!"

"Is she dangerous?" Abby asked, twisting her mallet absently in her palm.

"Matilda?" Charles asked. "Not at all."

"Violet said she threatened her," Abby pointed out.

His sigh came through the walkie-talkie. "You sure know how to take the fun out of a game."

"I'm still having fun," Abby said, striking the ball so it rolled directly through the fifth hoop.

Charles didn't cheer this time. The absence of his response was so unusual, Abby lifted the binoculars to check on him. He remained in the same place, staring at the empty bench swing. At last, he spoke softly and wearily. "I'll keep an eye on Matilda. Violet's fame has upset her, and she can be unpredictable when upset."

"Someone is leaving messages," Abby said. "The latest message accused someone of being a murderer. It was left in your room."

"That is odd," Charles admitted.

"There's no chance Matilda was murdered, is there?"

Charles shook his head, a sad expression crossing his face. "No. I was there. She was terribly sick. They called for a doctor and he prescribed her something, but she stopped taking it. I think she may have died partially from illness, and partially from a broken heart."

Abby hesitated, trying to sort out her thoughts. Charles had mentioned Matilda had a ring. Perhaps that ring was meant for Alice. Perhaps Matilda had proposed or was planning on proposing, but Alice broke up with her. Charles didn't know about Alice, and Abby wasn't about to out Matilda, but she needed to know about that ring. "Do you know what's keeping her here?" Abby asked.

Charles shook his head. "I haven't the slightest idea. Everyone she knew in life has moved on."

"What about the ring?" Abby pressured. "The one mentioned that she never took out of the box. Do you know where it is?"

Charles shook his head, a thoughtful expression crossing his face. "I believe she was buried with it."

Abby sucked in a sharp breath. If it turned out Matilda was the culprit, and the ring was what was keeping her here, she did not want to go digging up her grave to send her spirit on. She tightened her grip on her mallet. "Someone is leaving those messages. If it isn't you, Violet, or Matilda, who is it?"

"I don't know." Charles ran his fingers through his hair. "I suppose it *could* be Matilda, just trying to stir up trouble. She seems to take pleasure in getting an emotional reaction out of people."

"How do we get her to admit it?" Abby asked. "Or better yet, to stop?"

"Well…" Charles paced the length of the garden, wringing his hands and glancing over his shoulder toward the house, a worried expression on his face. He moved back toward Abby and asked, "Can you make my voice quieter?"

Abby turned the volume on the walkie-talkie down until she could barely hear it. She held it to her ear, motioning for Lucas to listen in as well. She was acutely aware of the salt necklace tucked under her sweater. If Charles tried anything, he wouldn't be able to place his hands on her. Which meant she could avoid his suspicion by leaving the salt gun clipped on her belt for the time being.

Lucas hurried across the croquet field, accidentally—or perhaps intentionally—kicking Abby's ball in the process. When he reached her side, he placed his ear next to hers, the walkie-talkie between them.

Charles spoke so quietly Abby was barely able to make out his next few words. "There wasn't a proper burial. There was…speculation concerning her relationship with god. The priest refused to bury her with the rest of the family. So my son buried her in the backyard."

Lucas looked down at his feet like he was going to be sick. "This backyard?"

"By that tree, I think."

Abby raised the binoculars in time to see Charles pointing to an old oak tree. He scratched his head, then pointed at a cherry tree on the opposite side of the yard. "Or maybe that one."

As much as Abby was more than a little creeped out by Matilda's presence, she felt for her. If Abby had been born in the 1800's, the rabbi would probably have refused to bury her too.

The sole of Lucas's shoes squeaked against the stone flower bed as he scraped one, then the other, against it. "That would explain why she's so unhappy all the time."

Abby lowered her binoculars, unable to stop herself from voicing her opinion. "If the manner of burial was important then there'd be a ton of atheist ghosts running around."

"Not necessarily," Lucas said. The breeze picked up, sending a shower of pine needles down around them. One of them stuck to Lucas's forehead, right between his eyebrows, exaggerating his frown until he resembled a cartoon grump. "Some spirits may need closure. If someone doesn't care if they're buried or not, that wouldn't be enough to keep them around. But for those of us who believe in a proper burial, it's important to do it right."

Abby considered that a moment. Since Chelsea died, she had spent a lot of time thinking about what happened after death and determined it was probably the same blissful nothingness felt in deep sleep. It wasn't scary, just sad when it happened to someone so young. After learning about ghosts, she had reassessed her beliefs. Now her theory was more along the lines of 'anything could happen'—including, apparently, ghosts being left behind because they weren't buried in the way they wanted.

She sighed. Maybe Charles *was* telling the truth. She needed to be prepared either way. "Okay, so if the improper burial is what's keeping Matilda here, what does that mean? We need to make a tombstone or—"

Lucas began to explain the precise details of a Protestant burial, which included words she had never heard before and didn't want to know the meaning of.

Eventually, Abby folded her arms across her chest and huffed. "What I'm hearing is that it's complicated and requires a priest, which none of us are."

"There is a priest buried in the church graveyard," Charles commented. "If he's still around, I believe he could perform the ritual."

"But we would still need to know where she's buried first," Lucas pointed out. "I don't know about you, but I sure as heck don't want to start digging this place up looking for a skeleton."

"Ditto," said Abby.

A back door slammed open. Harvey stepped out carrying a dark bag toward the dumpsters at the side of the house. She gave him a friendly wave, and he glared back in return. After he had properly disposed of the trash, he shouted across the backyard. "Doesn't look like you two are working."

"We are," Abby called back. "Charles here is telling us all kinds of helpful tips, in exchange for a game of croquet."

"Sure he is," Harvey replied, unlocking the door to a detached shed. Rows of gardening and repair tools lined one side, while mechanical tools and gas cans lined the other. He disappeared inside for several seconds, emerging with gardening gloves, a bucket, and large shears. He set his tools down while he secured the lock.

As he straightened, something slipped from his pocket. It gleamed as it fell onto a bed of grass.

Abby was about to tell him he dropped something, but as she moved closer, she realized what it was. An antique key, much like the ones she had, except it was solid black. She recalled seeing this key in Sam's hands on the day they arrived. The master key. The one that would let them into any room in the house, including Charles.

When Harvey's footsteps retreated around the side of the house, Abby crept forward and gently picked up the key.

"New plan." Slipping the key into her pocket, Abby returned to Lucas's side. "We're going to figure out how your sister's room got trashed. And—hopefully—who trashed it. Charles, we need your help."

Chapter Fifteen

The tantalizing scents of breakfast were starting to fade, but still strong enough to make Abby want to run to the kitchen to ask for leftovers. Instead, she lifted her feet and spun in the office's swivel chair, before turning back to the boring camera feed, waiting for Charles to make his move.

Most of the couples had left for the day, although the Magnolia room still had a 'do not disturb' sign on the knob. Harvey was outside, trimming the hedges (though the blinds were shut, she could hear his shears through the window, along with his occasional rebuffs to Cupid). Sam was cleaning up in the kitchen, while Susan paced the garden, shouting into her phone at someone who was apparently two-timing her. That meant the coast was totally clear. So what was taking Charles so long?

She was about to voice her concern when Lucas gasped and pointed to the monitor.

There, on the feed outside the Charles room, a glass vase

lifted into thin air, drifting slowly toward the door. Having instructed Charles to do just this, Abby had expected as much, but it was still rather alarming to see the object move under invisible hands. Not a trace of Charles was reflected on the security feed, but the glass remained firmly in view as it floated from one frame to the next.

"I knew it," Abby exclaimed. "There's no way I'd have missed a box of candles floating up this way. Whoever brought them in must have brought them in another way. Now for the real test—"

Abby watched the vase inch closer to the nearby wall. Ghosts could move through walls, but Abby doubted they could carry tangible objects through them. Still, she held her breath as the vase brushed the wall—and promptly shattered.

The sound echoed from upstairs, making Abby wince.

Lucas dropped to his knees, hiding under the desk.

"Okay, so, the ghost didn't bring the candles through the wall," Abby said, relieved. The thought of ghosts interacting with the real world was dangerous enough. "Which means they *must* have gotten them in some other way."

"Or they were already in the room, and you just missed them."

"They weren't," Abby stressed, realizing how ridiculous she sounded. But she had checked everywhere. If they hadn't come in through the door or the walls, how had they gotten in? She snapped her fingers. "The window."

Abby dashed out of the office and upstairs, avoiding the pile of broken glass as she headed to the Charles room.

"You might want to clean that up." Charles's voice came through the walkie-talkie, fading in and out as if the reception was bad.

Abby frowned, lifting the binoculars to her eyes. "Charles?"

She found him, sitting in his rocking chair, but he was faded and transparent, not like his usual self. "What happened?"

"Tired," said Charles, closing his eyes. "That vase took too much out of me. You know, I don't think I've ever—"

His sentence ended in static. Charles faded entirely out of sight. While Abby got the feeling he would return soon enough, his abrupt disappearance left an ominous emptiness behind. She lowered the binoculars, watching the unusually still rocking chair.

He was either innocent or an *exceptionally* good—and dangerous—actor.

Lucas's heavy breathing reached the landing behind her. She turned to find him holding a broom. "Next time you want to test your theory, give him a plastic spoon. Or anything that won't be this messy. I sure hope that vase wasn't valuable."

Abby nodded in agreement. She should have thought that through better. She had been so focused on proving her theory, it hadn't occurred to her the vase could break. "Thanks for cleaning it up. Keep watch for me, will you?"

Lucas nodded. "Hurry up. I'll make this sound if someone is coming—" He made a strange cawing sound, which was probably supposed to resemble a bird but sounded more like a cranky old cat.

"Just call my name," Abby replied, slipping the master key from her pocket. "Pretend you need help cleaning up."

Abby had barely turned toward the door to Charles when a door creaked open behind her.

"Ah, there you are." Dr. Greenwood stepped out, folding her arms across her chest. "I just called the front desk and no one answered."

"What is it?" Abby asked, craning her neck to see into Magnolia and scan for any signs of damage.

"I'd like a fresh pot of tea with cream, no sugar," she said.

"Excellent choice, Dr. Greenwood." Lucas beamed. "There's nothing quite like sitting with a hot cup of tea and a good book—like *Legendborn*, am I right?"

Dr. Greenwood studied Lucas with pursed lips. "Have you been spying on me?"

"N-no," Lucas stammered.

"We're paranormal investigators," Abby explained.

"She is," Lucas amended. "I'm between jobs at the moment."

"A paranormal investigator, huh?" Dr. Greenwood's flowy sleeves swished as she stepped toward Abby, her gaze sweeping over the binoculars around Abby's neck and the walkie-talkie at her hip.

"I actually just graduated with a degree in English literature," Lucas said, "and was hoping to apply to your English department this fall."

Dr. Greenwood continued to study Abby. "Are you attempting to contact the ghost of Violet Lovelace?"

"We've already contacted her," Abby said, wondering why an English professor would be interested in a ghost. Her mother, who was a psychology professor, was the biggest skeptic she knew. But Dr. Greenwood seemed genuinely curious, so Abby continued, "We actually don't think she's the one behind the latest hauntings. She hangs around out back, never comes inside. Or so the other ghosts tell us."

"Other ghosts?" Dr. Greenwood's eyes flashed. "You must tell me all about them."

Over Dr. Greenwood's shoulder, Lucas gave Abby an accusatory look and gesticulated that he would like to turn the conversation back to himself.

"I'm afraid I'm too busy at the moment." Abby faked a disappointed smile. "But Lucas can tell you all about it."

"Yes." Lucas stepped forward, nodding eagerly. "I'm not busy."

Dr. Greenwood turned to him. "Very well. Bring me my tea, and then tell me what you know about this place."

Abby pretended to busy herself by fidgeting with the antenna on her walkie-talkie until Dr. Greenwood returned to her room and the door clicked shut behind her. Lucas's footsteps were already retreating downstairs.

Silence filled the hall, broken only by the faint chirp of a bird through the window.

Abby raised the master key to the Charles room. It slipped easily into the lock. All it took was a sharp flick of her wrist and the door clicked open, spilling shadows onto the carpet.

She glanced at the camera, knowing her trespassing would be recorded. She told herself it wasn't *technically* trespassing since she worked there, and it wasn't like Michelle or David would press charges. But if Sam or Nathan saw the recording, that might be the final act that would get her and Lucas kicked out for good.

Taking a deep breath, Abby tiptoed into the room, letting the door creak shut behind her.

The room had clearly been occupied. Michelle's suitcase lay on the luggage rack, while David's lay on the floor, spilling several pairs of socks in assorted colors, all decorated with cartoon dogs. Coats hung in the wardrobe, a discarded towel draped over a chair, and an open wine bottle rested on the nightstand.

Sunlight crept through a thin break in the curtains, sparkling against the wine glasses and shimmering off something on the floor.

Abby knelt down and touched the shimmering substance. It clung to her fingers like sugar, but she would bet her wallet it was salt.

Michelle—or David—had circled the entire bed with it.

Abby brushed the salt from her fingers, smiling in approval. They had listened to her after all.

She continued a slow circle around the room, examining the mirror, shower, and bathroom. The most sinister thing she found was David's cologne, which came in a crystal package that looked like it cost a fortune.

Stepping back into the bedroom, Abby raised the binoculars to her eyes, doing a second, more intense scan of the room. Through the lenses, layers of various wallpaper peeked out from behind one another, the room transforming into a mosaic of history, with ghosts of a bed here and there, and various paintings overlapping in different positions. Only the trim remained the same, stern and direct as it framed the ceiling and floor of the room, breaking only at the doors and—oddly—behind the wardrobe.

Abby lowered and raised the binoculars, frowning.

The sleek mahogany wardrobe looked as if it had been built for the room, matching the bed frame and desk. But through the binoculars, it was barely more than a wisp. Letting the binoculars hang loose around her neck, Abby stepped forward and gave the wardrobe a shove, wondering if perhaps there had once been a door behind it.

To her surprise, it rolled easily, on hidden wheels that scraped against the carpet. She had to lift a hand to stop it from crashing into the far wall. Once she had the wardrobe under control, she turned back to the wall behind it, expecting to find an old boarded-up door covered in dust. Instead, the same burgundy wallpaper filled the space. The wallpaper ended several centimeters from the floor, disappearing into a small shadowy crack.

Sure enough, there was a door: a hidden door, painted to blend in with the wall.

There was no knob or handle, but as Abby ran her hands along the wallpaper, she felt the faint outline, a hairline thick.

Her fingers tingled with the thrill of discovery as she pressed against the door. It didn't budge. It had probably been sealed over years ago, but she was too curious to let it go. She dropped to her knees and slipped her fingers under the slight gap between the door and the floorboard. They barely fit, but she was able to grasp the other side.

Wriggling her fingers, she tugged on the door, but it wouldn't open. She slid her fingers back and placed her palms on the door, shoving as hard as she could. She toppled forward as the door inched open, retreating into the dark space beyond.

Peering cautiously around the edge, she saw only darkness. Cold damp air brushed her cheeks. It smelled old and musty, with a faint hint of something chemical.

As her eyes adjusted, she noticed a stairwell a few feet away.

So this was how Matilda or Charles brought in the candles without being caught on camera. Abby was willing to bet a coffee—maybe even a pizza—that this would lead to the office. Of course there would be a hidden door behind one of those bookshelves.

She did a quick sweep for ghosts. Seeing only darkness, she slipped out her phone and turned on the flashlight.

A narrow set of dusty wooden stairs stared back at her, the edges slightly splintered. She stepped carefully, clutching the wall with her free hand for support in case the stairs broke under her. The first step held fast. The second wobbled.

The third step creaked loudly and splintered in half, causing her to gasp. She reached both hands out, gripping the stairwell while adjusting her feet to more solid wood.

Something thumped down the stairs, crashing at the bottom, where its faint light was all but lost against the shadows around a curve.

Abby reached a shaky hand to the binoculars around her neck, reassuring herself they were still safe. Next, she checked her belt, where she felt the salt gun and walkie-talkie, ghostly antenna still intact. Moving on to her pockets, she felt her wallet and a few loose coins, but her phone was mysteriously absent.

Right, she had been using it as a flashlight.

Damn.

Abby glanced back at the glowing light and winced, hoping her phone case was strong enough to withstand that. She doubted it was.

Beside her phone, something else glowed faintly in the dark. It looked suspiciously like the LED candles they had decorated Michelle and David's room with.

She had half a mind to turn back and get Lucas, but the stairs creaked behind her. A dark shadow filled her vision. Someone reached toward her.

She opened her mouth to scream, but they shoved a cloth against her lips.

Images of being strangled by lace flooded her vision, and she lashed out, shoving hard. But her hand made contact with someone solid, someone who said *ooph*.

Abby stumbled backward, and had the scary sensation of falling into darkness.

Chapter Sixteen

"Abby!" Lucas shouted from somewhere far away. Or maybe it was close, she couldn't be sure.

"Abby." Mina's voice this time. She sounded worried.

Why was Mina here? Abby struggled to think, struggled to blink, as her mind slowly came back to her.

She was lying on something hard. No, soft; soft, but firm. A bed. Maybe she really was dreaming.

She blinked. This time, the world came into view, albeit a bit blurry.

Lucas and Mina hovered over her, their faces caricatures of worry. Abby would have laughed, if she could get her muscles to move.

"You—" She pointed at Lucas, licking her lips, having trouble forming the words. Her tongue was heavy, with a metallic taste to it. "You look like that grumpy cat meme."

Lucas's frown only deepened. Mina let out a sigh of relief,

before turning to Lucas and nodding. "You know, I see it."

"This isn't a time for jokes." Lucas ran his fingers over his short hair. "Do you realize I thought you'd died?"

Abby frowned as her surroundings came into focus. The dark vampiric furniture of Charles stared down at her—and, over Lucas's shoulder, a worried Michelle stared at her as well.

Abby attempted to sit up. That was a struggle. She made it to her elbows, then crashed against the pillows. Her muscles felt weak, but nothing appeared to be broken. "If you thought I was dead, why did you put me in bed?"

"Told you we should have called an ambulance." Michelle retreated toward the hidden door and began to pace, as if standing guard. Cupid followed her, his tail wagging back and forth as he left damp pawprints on the burgundy carpet.

"Before that," Lucas said. "When I first found you."

"How did you find me?" Abby glanced at the window, where storm clouds drifted over the front lawn. "And how long have I been unconscious?"

"Over an hour." Mina tenderly handed Abby a glass of water.

That long? It felt like two seconds. Abby sipped the water, relief washing over her as it dulled the bad dry taste in her mouth. Once she had drained most of the glass, she handed it back to Mina, who placed it on the nightstand. "What happened?"

Lucas and Mina exchanged worried glances. "We were hoping you could tell us."

"I heard a sound," Lucas continued. "Like a crash. You didn't answer. I tried to come in, but the door was locked."

"I didn't lock it."

Lucas nodded, leaning forward in the chair he had clearly

moved from the desk to the side of Abby's bed. "I figured as much. I waited a few minutes—thinking you were up to something—but after a while, I started to get worried. I found Sam, who used their key to get in. We found you passed out on the floor by the wardrobe."

"There's a—"

"Secret passage behind it, I know. It was cracked open when we found you." Lucas fidgeted with the rolled-up sleeves of his sweater and rested his hand on his knee, which was bouncing with nervous energy. He must have really been worried. Abby had only seen him vibrate like this before big tests or when he was sure his parents were going to ground him. "David and Sam are going to board it up."

"Where does it go?" Abby asked.

"Out back," Mina said, leaning against the bed at Abby's side. "And get this—it also goes up to Violet. Sam and the rest of the staff didn't know anything about it."

"Well someone does," Abby replied. "They used it to bring in those candles. And probably the candy hearts, too."

"I contacted a priest," Lucas said. "He can be here Monday. We can get Matilda put to rest before she hurts anyone else."

Abby shook her head and winced as the pain increased. She would not be doing that again any time soon. "I don't think it was Matilda."

Lucas frowned. "What do you mean?"

"When I was in that passage, whoever attacked me, it wasn't a ghost," Abby said, trying to make sense of her muddled thoughts by thinking out loud. "I felt something solid. And they put a cloth over my mouth, but I don't think they were trying to strangle me. It tasted funny. And I fell asleep so quickly, almost like—"

"They wanted to knock you out," Mina deduced, folding her arms across her chest. Her face took on a pinched expression.

Lucas scratched the back of his head. "Are you sure?"

Abby nodded, wincing as the movement aggravated her headache.

"Told you we should've called the police." Michelle paused her pacing to glare at the wardrobe.

Cupid gave a joyful bark and playfully nudged her hand.

"No," Abby insisted, imagining the humiliation of being questioned by an officer on sneaking into a room to look for ghosts. At best, it would be a complete waste of time. At worst, she could end up in jail asking her mother for bail.

Cupid whined and sat down, clearly thinking the 'no' was for him.

Sighing, Michelle patted his head, picked up a ball of David's socks, and tossed it across the room. Cupid chased it eagerly, his pale tail swaying in the dim light.

"Sorry," Abby said. "I'm fine. Tell Sam not to board it up yet."

Lucas frowned. "Why?"

"Whoever attacked me might come back. We should put a camera up, see if we can find out who they are and what they want."

"No," Mina said sharply. "It's too dangerous."

"I don't think whoever attacked me wanted to hurt me," Abby explained. "Just scare me."

"Well they certainly accomplished that." Mina rapped the back of her fist against the side of the bed, rattling the frame.

Abby nodded toward Lucas. "See if you can talk to Charles. Ask if he saw anything."

Lucas glanced around. "Where are the binoculars?"

"I don't know," Abby said, a sinking feeling forming in her chest. "I had them with me in the passageway, when I lost consciousness."

"Do you think they fell?" Mina asked.

Abby shrugged. She peeled back the covers and glanced down at her waist. The walkie-talkie was missing from her belt. She shut her eyes and let out an agitated sound. "No. I think they were stolen."

Chapter
Seventeen

Abby's headache persisted as the sky darkened, and her muscles soon joined in. The constant hum of the radiator kept her company as she slipped in and out of dreamless sleep. At one point, she woke to the warmth of Mina's smooth hands brushing her hair out of her face. She pretended to stay asleep so the gentle strokes would continue, but eventually, Mina caught on.

"Lucas brought you painkillers."

That was enough to get Abby to open her eyes and struggle to sit up. The motion caused her to wince, her entire upper body feeling like she had fallen out of a moving vehicle.

"Careful," Mina said, supporting Abby into a gentle seat with her back firmly pressed against the pillows.

She handed her two small pills and a glass of water, which Abby managed to gulp down quickly, realizing as soon as it touched her lips that she needed more. "This is the best water I've ever tasted."

"You're just dehydrated."

"You sure? It's not some fancy spring water?"

Mina bit her lip, likely in an attempt to stop the smirk spreading across her features. It didn't work. "It came from Michelle, so yeah, it's fancy. But no water is *that* good."

Mina leaned forward, her graceful fingers massaging Abby's forehead, as if checking for some problem area she could physically remove. It was not unpleasant. "How are you feeling?"

Abby delayed her response, savoring Mina's touch until the motion stilled. "Like I want to stay in bed and watch TV all day."

Mina lifted the blanket that pooled at Abby's side from the duvet, draping the soft wool over Abby's shoulders. "There's not much day left, but I think we can make that happen."

Abby settled deep into the blanket, slipping her hands under the duvet cover at her waist, until she was cocooned in warmth. As comfortable as it was, she doubted she could fully relax after what had just happened. She ran her thumb across her belt loop where the walkie-talkie usually rested. "We need to find our equipment."

Mina let out a heated sigh. "*You* need to stay in bed."

"But what if whoever attacked me plans to destroy them?" Abby's heartbeat quickened as she realized she had no idea how to replace her equipment. Her only chance at seeing ghosts—at seeing *Chelsea*—was getting her binoculars back.

Mina sat on the edge of the bed, far enough from Abby that their limbs didn't touch. She leaned forward and spoke in a soft tentative whisper that was unusual for her. "Would that really be a bad thing?"

The heat cranked up, fluttering the velvet curtains until their shadows swayed across the foot of the bed.

Abby's throat burned with both the aftereffects of whatever had been used to knock her unconscious and the sounds of protest spilling through her lips. "Yes! We came here to catch a ghost!"

"*You* came here to catch a ghost," Mina corrected.

Any other time, Abby would have felt guilty at the prodding reminder that Mina had come here to spend time with *her*, but currently Abby was too tired, and too achy, to feel multiple emotions at once.

"I promised Sam," she insisted. "And I can help them! Matilda deserves a proper burial. And Violet deserves to be reunited with her fiancé."

Mina winced, sliding away from Abby and Abby realized that she had been shouting. She opened her mouth to apologize, but her throat stung too much, as if each word had scraped her throat on its way out. She sighed. The truth was, she *loved* talking to ghosts—hearing their stories, peeking into a world beyond death—it fueled her rebellious spirit, making her feel like she was bending the rules against nature itself. She couldn't begin to explain how thrilling it was to commune with a spirit the world had forgotten.

"That may be true." Mina continued in her careful tone that reminded Abby of a psychiatrist speaking to a very anxious and unpredictable patient. The scowl on her face undid any effect her tone achieved. "But it's not your responsibility to help the dead."

Abby pulled the blanket tighter around her, wishing she had a way to make Mina understand. Of course it wasn't her *responsibility* to help ghosts move on, just like it wasn't her responsibility to help Lucas get a job, or make sure the kids she performed magic tricks for enjoyed their birthday parties. But she *wanted* to help. Speaking with Violet and Charles—and even Matilda—kindled a desire to help them be happy. At least, as happy as the dead could be. She couldn't explain it, but it made her feel a little less helpless—and gave her life a little more meaning.

After a painful fit of coughing, Abby choked out the words, "I *want* to help."

Mina's eyes narrowed, but she nodded, sliding back up to press her shoulder against Abby's. "We'll look for the equipment. *Tomorrow*. As long as you rest tonight. Deal?"

Abby wanted to argue, but considering the mere act of sitting up in bed was this draining, she doubted she'd make it very far. With a sigh, she sank deeper under the covers. "Deal."

Mina's warm fingers returned to her forehead, accompanied by a soft brush of her lips. Smiling, Abby drifted off to sleep.

WHEN SHE WOKE an hour later, Mina was still at her side, watching silent videos on her phone. Lucas sat in a nearby armchair, drawing in his sketchbook, his laptop giving off an eerie blue glow on the desk beside him.

Abby kissed Mina's cheek, pleased to see she evoked a smile before she slipped out of bed and into the luxurious bathroom. She managed to shower and change into clean clothes, but then she crawled back in bed, her energy fading as her cough returned.

"Are you sure you don't need a doctor?" Lucas asked, handing Abby a steaming mug of tea.

She shook her head, taking a tentative sip. The tea was citrusy and honey flavored—not quite as sweet as she preferred, but it soothed her throat and for that she was appreciative. "I'm feeling better every second."

Mina frowned. "If that cough doesn't go away, we're taking you to urgent care."

"You two"—Abby coughed—"worry too much."

"*You* worry us too much," Lucas countered, before taking a seat on the foot of the bed with a sigh. "Now, do you know who attacked you? And why?"

"I'm not sure," Abby admitted. "They were definitely alive. And they took my phone and equipment."

Lucas shook his head. "They didn't take your phone. David found it in the passageway. What's left of it anyway."

Mina moved to the dresser and picked up Abby's phone. She placed it gently on the nightstand so Abby could see the series of large cracks through the screen.

Abby plugged it in anyway, hoping it would at least charge. The screen remained black. She leaned back against the pillows with a heavy sigh. There went her plan of getting a website set up for her new paranormal investigation agency. The money she'd been saving for that would have to go to a new phone. Then again, a website wouldn't matter if she lost her only way of communicating with ghosts. "But David didn't find the binoculars or walkie-talkie?"

"No," Lucas said gently. "He didn't. I think you're right. Whoever attacked you must have taken them."

"Why?" Mina asked with a shrug. "Why would someone take those and not her phone or wallet?"

"Because they knew what they were," Abby theorized. "They knew what they could do. They wanted to talk to a ghost."

Lucas scratched the back of his head. "Or maybe a ghost

knows something about them, and they didn't want us talking to them."

"The last message said 'murderer,' right?" Mina twisted her thumb ring. "What if a ghost was trying to warn us? That someone here is a murderer."

"The only ghost who could have any connection to the living is Violet." Lucas's eyebrows arched together, indicating he was thinking deeply. "And the only person old enough to have known her while she was alive is Harvey."

"Wasn't Nathan here the night of the fire?" Mina asked.

"Yeah, but he was six," Lucas said. "You don't think he murdered Violet?"

Mina shrugged as if to say 'anything is possible.' "I don't like that guy."

"He curls his 'm's," Abby said. "Like the messages."

"The *one* message," Lucas said thoughtfully, holding up his pencil. "The one on the mirror. What if *he* wrote that message *to* Violet?"

"He thinks she's a murderer?" Mina raised an eyebrow.

"No, that message didn't have a curlicue. It was only the one on the mirror. The one that said *join me*."

"You think Nathan wrote that?"

"Maybe." Lucas tapped his pencil against his lips. "Maybe he's been communicating with Violet. And she's been communicating back."

"Violet said she didn't leave any messages," Abby said, her thoughts moving slower than usual. She felt like there was some vital piece of information right in front of her, but she was feeling for it in the dark.

"She also said Matilda didn't want her in the house," Mina pointed out. "She could have been too afraid to take credit for the messages."

"Or she might not have any memory of it," Lucas added, rubbing his stubbly chin.

"Or Matilda wrote those messages pretending to be Violet," Abby theorized.

Mina pinched her forehead like she was thinking so hard it pained her. She shook her head. "This is really spiraling out of control."

"Where's Michelle?" Abby asked, realizing the room was much cleaner. She glanced at the luggage rack and saw it was empty.

"She and David are staying at the inn down the road," Lucas said.

They must have left while she was in the shower. She was really off her game today, not noticing something as obvious as that.

"Did they board up the passage?" Abby asked.

"They boarded the inside, but left the back door open so we can look around when you feel up to it," Mina explained. "But no one can get in our rooms tonight."

"Not that it matters to us," Lucas added, frowning in Abby's direction. "I've made arrangements for the three of us to stay at Sam's place."

The pillows scratched against the back of Abby's neck as she adjusted her position to get a good look at both her companions. "I'd rather stay here."

"You've got to be kidding me." Lucas got to his feet and threw his hand to his face, slapping his cheek as if trying to wake himself up from a bad dream.

"It's not safe," Mina insisted, her warm brown eyes filled with tender concern.

Abby gave her a look, torn between annoyance and amusement. Mina made a living off jumping from buildings and running through fires—things far more dangerous than ghosts. "Since when have you cared about safety?"

"Since you nearly *died*."

Mina's words hung in the air, the weight of them emphasized by the abrupt halt of the radiator.

"I'm fine," Abby insisted, which was becoming more and more true. Each second, her headache faded a bit more, and the time between her fits of coughing grew longer.

Mina's shoulders stiffened, her fists clenched. "You were *attacked*."

Abby's mug clanked softly against the nightstand as she set it down and maneuvered so her feet dangled off the side of the bed. "We've all been attacked. It sort of comes with the job. Just like stunt work comes with risks of injury, ghost hunting comes with risks of ghost attacks."

"But this time it wasn't a ghost." Mina turned her gaze toward Lucas, eyes narrowed as if imploring him to take her side.

Lucas gulped, tugging at the collar of his shirt. He licked his lips, refusing to meet Abby's gaze.

The satin sheets scratched against Abby's palms as she clenched the edge of the bed. "If you two want to go, then go. I'm staying until the job is done."

Mina looked as if she were about to argue, but Lucas spoke first. "Technically, we came here to prove if this place was haunted. Which we did. I say we say job well done, collect our paycheck, and get out of here."

"We're getting paid to *stop* the hauntings," Abby said. "What difference does it make if someone living is involved?"

"A huge difference!" Mina exclaimed, her forehead wrinkled with worry. "You fight ghosts, not people."

"Ghosts are people."

"We have weapons against ghosts," Lucas continued hesitantly. "What do we have that stops people?"

"Walls." Abby pointed to the boarded-up wall behind the dresser. "And cameras."

"Those do not stop people, they deter people," Lucas said pointedly.

Mina returned to Abby's side, her glossy lips quivering. "What if whoever attacked you comes back?"

Abby met her gaze, pleading with her to see how determined she was to see this through. "We catch them. Set your phone up so it films that passage. We can take turns staying awake. Again, I don't think anyone wants to hurt us. If they wanted our equipment, they got what they came for. If they wanted to scare us away, then we *have* to stay to make sure they don't do whatever they're planning on doing next—which is probably going after whichever spirit left those messages."

Lucas shook his head, signaling he didn't agree. He looked at Mina, clearly expecting her to have a strong counterargument.

Mina's rings clattered quietly as she tapped her ghoulish fingernails rhythmically against her elbows. At last, her lips pressed into a determined line. "Fine."

Lucas's jaw dropped. "Fine?"

Mina nodded, her eyes cooling to their usual warmth. "I'll stay."

A grin broke across Abby's face, causing Mina's lips to twitch in a way that meant she was trying to keep herself from smiling.

"Under one condition," Mina continued, "you are not to leave the room without one of us under any circumstance. Got it?"

"Promise."

"For the record, she has about a sixty percent ratio of keeping her promises," Lucas chimed in.

Abby leaned back against her pillow with a heavy sigh.

Mina's frown deepened. Her fingers reached out, finding Abby's almost magnetically. Their soft warmth sent a soothing feeling up Abby's arm, which settled in her heart, causing her to relax.

"Well, you better keep this one," Mina said softly.

"For you, I will," Abby promised. This time, she meant it.

Lucas cleared his throat. "Well, I guess I'll see you in the morning, then."

"You're not staying?"

"Nope." Lucas shut his laptop, folded it under his arm, picked up his sketchbook, and headed toward the door. "I'm getting a good night's sleep in Sam's safe, secret-passage-free, house."

As he stepped into the hall, he called over his shoulder, "You two keep each other safe."

"We will," Mina and Abby called in unison.

Lucas gave Abby a final disapproving look, shrugged, and moved deeper into the hall. The door slammed shut behind him.

In the silence that followed, Abby noticed the windows had grown dark, with only the faintest twinkle of string lights in the distance.

Noticing the same thing, Mina turned to Abby with a look of alarm. "It's after sunset."

Abby blinked. "Are you expecting a meeting with a vampire?"

Mina's eyebrows drew together in her unamused look. "It's Friday. Don't you light candles?"

Abby's eyes widened. "Who told you that?"

"You did. The story with the mouse."

Abby shut her eyes, remembering how—during one of their recent phone calls—she had shared a story of how her childhood cat had batted a toy into the Shabbat candles and consequently sent a flaming mechanical mouse around the kitchen table. The char marks were still there. How was it that, just days ago, she had felt so close to Mina despite them being miles apart? And now, when she was mere inches away, she felt more distant than ever.

Abby swallowed. "I forgot about that. I haven't lit them in years. Not since I moved out of my parents' place."

Mina brushed a thick strand of hair behind her triple-pierced ear. "Well, I brought some candles. I thought we could light them. I should have asked. I feel like an idiot."

"No, that's really thoughtful," Abby assured her. That warm, tingly sensation spread from her heart down to her fingertips as they reached for Mina's. "Let's light them."

Mina's expression hardened as her dark brown eyes bore into Abby's. "Don't pity me."

"I'm not." Abby traced her thumb along the inside of Mina's wrist. Somewhere down the hall, a door creaked open and shut, as a couple teased each other on their way down-stairs. She wished that ease would return between her and Mina. Sighing, she tossed aside her blanket and moved closer to Mina, until she was inches from being pressed against her side. "I screwed up."

Mina raised an eyebrow. "By getting yourself knocked out or by losing your ghost-hunting equipment?"

"Those too," Abby admitted. "But I was talking about with you. I wanted this weekend to be special. I wanted it to be romantic."

A smile danced across Mina's face. "There's still time."

Abby's gnawing guilt burst into something warm and hopeful that fluttered in her heart like confetti. "I'm glad you stuck around. I'm just not sure I'm ready for all that romance."

Mina stiffened. "Are you saying you just want to be friends?"

"No," Abby assured her, relieved that Mina's grip relaxed—both because she knew Mina still had feelings for her, and because Mina had been cutting the circulation from her knuckles. "I'm saying I want to take things slow. If that's okay with you. I haven't been on many dates. And I've only ever been in one serious relationship and you've been in so many—"

Mina laughed a sharp disbelieving laugh, deep and unrestrained. "What gave you that impression?"

Abby blinked. "You slept with Michelle's roommate. And you said you've dated plenty of people."

"Yeah, *dated*." Mina waved her free hand. "And sure, I've had a few one-night stands I'm not proud of, but I've only been in four and a half relationships, none of which have lasted more than a few months."

Abby laughed, giddy from the relief surging through her. "What's a half relationship?"

"He thought we were dating, I thought we were friends with benefits." Mina shrugged. "Honestly, this romantic thing is pretty new for me too. It's been a few years since I liked anyone as much as I like you."

"What happened to the last person?"

"That's a story for another day." Mina sighed. "Needless to say, they're not around, and I am very clearly falling for you."

"Falling...*in love*?" Abby bolted into a seated position, staring at Mina's warm brown eyes. They gleamed with amusement.

"I said *falling*," Mina said playfully. She ran her thumb across Abby's knuckles, sending pleasant shivers up Abby's arm. "Don't get too far ahead of yourself. If I didn't like you so damn much, I wouldn't be here."

Abby felt her cheeks warm with a blush. "I'm falling for you too. I just need time to get used to this—" She lifted their intertwined hands.

The electric lamp illuminated Mina's face, so Abby could see every expression flicker across her features. They passed so rapidly, she only managed to deduce a few—approval, calculation, and, lastly, acceptance. "When you say you want to take things slow, do you mean physically, emotionally, or publicly—as in announcing it on social media and whatnot?"

"All of the above," Abby admitted, feeling guilty.

Mina leaned toward her, her breath tickling Abby's nose. "Is kissing okay?"

"More than okay," Abby breathed, her eyes fluttering shut as she closed the distance between them.

Mina's lips brushed against hers, soft and firm and tantalizing as she pulled her closer, deepening the kiss. Abby's heart fluttered. Her cheeks warmed with desire as she moved her own lips faster, dancing against Mina's. Mina's kisses were strong and passionate, nothing like Chelsea's gentle pecks. Mina kissed with more than just her mouth, her entire body was alive with passion as she leaned into Abby, wrapping her hands through her hair and around her waist.

The door opened.

Abby was vaguely aware of Lucas standing at the edge of her vision, clearing his throat, as Mina slowly, tenderly, brushed her lips against Abby's before breaking the kiss.

Her absence left a cold, empty feeling, as if she had stepped out into a winter storm without her coat. Every part of her wanted to grab Mina and pull her back into her arms.

But Mina was already out of reach, having moved to lean against the foot of the bed.

"I thought you were leaving," Abby said. The words came out through more of a pout than she intended.

"I am," Lucas said in a rush, "but I ran into Nathan and he—"

"—wants to apologize." Nathan stepped into the room, wringing his hands in an awkward manner. "I hope I've not offended you in some way?"

It was a struggle to turn her attention from Mina's attractive smirk to the stern man in the doorframe. Abby rubbed the back of her thumb against her lower lip, attempting to subdue her own smile. It had the opposite effect, strengthening her desire for Mina's lips to return to that very spot, and making her grin even wider.

Instead, she attempted to compose herself by tucking her hair behind her ears and staring at Nathan's very un-sexy polka-dot tie. "You haven't."

Nathan nodded, as if he had anticipated this answer. "Then why did you directly ignore my advice from before?"

"I didn't bother the guests," Abby insisted, trying to figure out what advice he was referring to that she may have accidentally ignored. "I haven't posted anything online about this place."

That last part was technically true, minus a few selfies on her personal account, but she doubted Nathan cared about that. He hadn't wanted her to post anything about the place being haunted before running it by Sam, and she hadn't. Not since their last conversation, at least. She hoped he hadn't found her post from the carriage ride, where she had posted a picture of Violet Lovelace, asking if anyone knew the identity of her boyfriend. It had barely a dozen likes and not a single response.

"I said *entertain* the guests, not scare them," he continued as if Abby hadn't spoken. He moved deeper into the room, brushing his thumb along the edge of the wardrobe before opening it and inspecting the inside. Even though Michelle and David's things were no longer there, it felt like an invasion of privacy.

Abby studied him, noticing his restlessness as he moved, the slight stubble sprouting on his chin. Lamplight sparkled off his impeccably clean shoes—seriously, there's no way he's been outside in those things. He must have changed when he came inside. Abby realized—with a sudden jolt of alertness—that he could have been the one who had attacked her in the passage.

The door to the wardrobe groaned shut as Nathan turned back to Abby, his thin lips pressed together in a narrow line. "I have to say, finding that passage is impressive work. I had completely forgotten it existed."

Abby leaned back, studying his expression. His words seemed genuine, not overly calculated or intense, but tossed out with the same arrogant nonchalance as when they had first met. He was either telling the truth or such a practiced liar that he delivered falsehoods with ease. She wished she had fought her attacker harder, punching them in the jaw or eye or stealing a fistful of hair—something to leave at least the slightest indication of a physical altercation.

"But an attack is a bit too 'horror' for our image," Nathan continued, tapping his right temple with his index finger as if that would make his thoughts come faster. "Our ghosts are more like Casper—friendly and playful. This passage could have led you to a nice fireside chat with Violet. Think about that when you write your story."

"There is no story," Mina snapped. In her combat boots, she was an inch or two taller than him—which she used to her advantage. She shoved a finger in his face, stopping mere inches from his eye.

"Oh, there better be a story," Nathan said, his expression hardening as his cheeks grew red. "If I find that you've been snooping around with ulterior motives, you better believe you'll be slapped so hard with legal fees you won't be able to afford a house until you're fifty."

As much as Abby considered that an empty threat—she had little interest in owning a house—the defensiveness behind it was thick. Nathan was hiding something; something important to him that he *really* didn't want Abby to find out.

"Abby was attacked!" Mina countered. "In *your* hotel, which has an undisclosed passage into a guest room. How many esteemed guests have slept here, unknowing that someone could walk in on them—or spy on them—at any second? You're lucky we haven't called the police."

Abby expected Nathan to balk—or at least flinch—at Mina's accusation, but his face twisted into an unnerving grin as if he were enjoying it. "And you are lucky I haven't called them on you for you illegally occupying this room."

"This is my sister's room," Lucas said. "She knows they're here."

"She and her husband checked out hours ago," Nathan said, his smug expression growing as he puffed out his chest. "Unless you plan on paying, I suggest you take my advice— say nothing about the passage or anything you've seen here unless you've cleared it with *me* first. Not a member of my staff, *me*." He pointed to himself as if Abby didn't know who he was referring to.

"Is that a threat?" Mina all but growled.

"An invitation," Nathan clarified. His canine-revealing grin said otherwise. "Tonight, this room is on us. I don't expect to see you loitering in the halls or speaking with the other guests, or sticking around a second past ten tomorrow morning—or I'll consider it trespassing. Understood?"

Abby assumed the question was rhetorical—there wasn't really any way to misunderstand that.

But Lucas nodded, clutching his laptop to his chest like a frightened high school student being chewed out by the principal. "Understood, sir."

"And what are you going to do about that?" Mina asked, pointing toward the secret passage.

Nathan shrugged. "It's been boarded up."

"No thanks to you." Mina huffed.

"Lucky for you, it's no longer your concern what I do with *my* property." Reaching for the door, he turned back to Abby, his slick gaze making contact with hers. "Good night. Sleep well."

"Oh, we will." Mina stormed toward the door as if to shut it in his face, but it was closed by the time she arrived. She slammed the lock in place as his footsteps retreated down the hall. "I hate that guy. He didn't care at all that you were attacked. It's like he thinks you made it up or something."

"Oh, I think he believes it." Abby rubbed her thumb across the luxury comforter. "I think he may have been the one who attacked me."

The looks of surprise Mina and Lucas gave her were so

wide-eyed and comical, she wished she had a camera to capture the moment. But they soon contorted to looks of horror.

"Seriously?" Lucas asked. "Why?"

Abby sighed. She couldn't pinpoint why, exactly, she thought Nathan had attacked her. Only that *someone* had, and that Nathan had recently changed his shoes, which made it seem like he had something on his previous shoes that he wanted to hide. "That's the part I'm still trying to figure out."

"Are you sure you still want to stay here?" Mina asked.

Abby nodded. "Absolutely. Where are those candles you mentioned? Let's light them."

Lucas scratched the back of his neck, looking like he was working out a complicated math problem. "I guess I'll get my things. After that, there's no way I'm letting you two sleep here alone tonight. One of us should keep watch at all times."

Abby supposed he was right. She flashed Mina an apologetic smile. So much for a romantic evening.

Staying alive was more important.

Chapter Eighteen

Abby couldn't remember the last time she had woken up this early. Judging by the grumbles from her companions, it had been a while since they had been up hours before dawn too. As she crept out the back door, porch light flooded her vision, stinging her eyes and unleashing a string of whispered curses from Mina.

Abby hurried to the far end of the porch, cold air stinging her lungs. She glanced at the dark windows above, hoping they didn't wake Nathan. While they weren't technically breaking any of his rules yet, they were about to. It was best he slept through that part.

As she moved out of the zone of the automatic porch light, it shut off as abruptly as it had turned on. Darkness settled around her shoulders like a cape. She crouched behind a table, watching the windows. After several seconds of darkness, she risked moving forward.

Stepping off the stone patio, she moved on to frosted grass, which crunched under her sneakers.

In the starlight, the garden took on an ethereal winter glow. Trees stood impeccably still, their branches budding with tiny icicles. Even the bench swing didn't dare move, resting silently between tired chains.

Abby stayed as close to the house as the hedges would allow, moving slowly toward the left.

"There," Mina grunted, attempting to point toward the house with two steaming mugs in her hands. She ended up using her elbow. "Behind that planter."

Abby frowned at the towering spiky plant. Its leaves reached over her head while the stone planter was larger than her nightstand. It must weigh at least one hundred pounds. There was no way she could lift that.

"Are you sure?"

Mina took a sip of coffee. "I had to move that damn thing out of the way so David could get out, then put it back. It's got my sweat all over it. I'm *not* looking forward to moving it again."

"We'll help," Lucas offered, sipping tea from his thermos. Bundled in his winter gloves, hat, and scarf, he was a bit over-dressed for the weather but would be fine if they ended up skiing.

Mina handed Abby her mug, downed the rest of her coffee, and set the empty mug on the base of a holly bush. She rubbed her palms together. "I got it."

Abby sipped a cup of rich hot chocolate as Mina headed toward the planter. Even through her leather jacket, Abby could see her muscles tense as she dropped into a deadlift stance and lifted the entire planter with ease, setting it a few feet away.

Abby clapped her free hand against her mug. "That took a lot less time than I thought it would take."

Mina rolled her shoulders as she turned back toward Abby, a flirtatious gleam in her eye. "Sorry to cut the show short. But I'm ready for more coffee."

As Abby moved forward to inspect the door to the passage, Mina brushed her fingers over Abby's shoulder. It was such a quick light graze, Abby had no explanation for why it made her heart flutter so much.

She turned to the back wall, searching for a door. In the shadows, there was nothing to differentiate a door from the bare stretch of wall. "Where—"

"I got you." Lucas slipped his phone from his pocket and turned on the flashlight. Cupping his hand over the top, he directed the light toward the back wall.

Abby blinked. The pale exterior glistened in the light, but there was no door. She'd opened her mouth to say so when Mina once again placed her hand on Abby's shoulder, more firmly this time.

"Look for the latch," Mina suggested. "The door is hidden."

Consumed with thoughts of Mina's affection, Abby didn't hesitate to reach out and touch the wall. The cold surface sent chills up her arm. She ran her fingers at the general height where a doorknob would be until she felt a small divot. Reaching inside, she felt a latch and pulled.

The latch clicked. Under Abby's guidance, the door creaked open, sliding inward, toward a dark set of stairs.

"That is scary as hell," Lucas said.

"See if you can find the binoculars or walkie-talkie," Abby instructed, stepping inside. As she did, she momentarily cut off most of Lucas's phone light, engulfing herself in the dark narrow hall that she had been attacked in mere hours ago. "And let's make sure no one's here."

"I'll go first," Mina offered. This time, her hand went to Abby's side as she gently guided Abby back into the garden and stepped inside. She took out her phone with its faded purple cover, turned on the light, and hurried up the steps in a yellow glow. The light grew fainter as she climbed until it disappeared entirely, the gentle thumping of her footsteps fading with it.

"It's odd," Lucas said, inspecting the door as he stroked his chin. "Those stairs look old, but this door is made of vinyl."

"So?"

"So, even if this passage is a hundred years old, the door is made of the same vinyl siding as the rest of the house. That wasn't made until the late 1950s."

"How do you know this?" Abby asked.

"College," Lucas said simply. "I took an intro to architecture class. Not only that, but vinyl siding needs to be updated every fifteen to thirty years. This looks like it was updated recently— five years ago, at most."

"What are you trying to say?" Abby asked, hoping Lucas had a point.

"Whoever had the siding redone definitely knew about this door. If they hadn't, it would have been sealed over."

"Nathan," Abby said, strengthening her suspicion of his involvement. "Why would he want a secret passageway?"

Lucas rubbed the back of his neck. "Beats me."

At the same time, a sharp crack of wood came from inside the passage, higher up.

She suddenly had a horrifying vision in which the stairs collapsed under Mina and she fell, broken and bruised in a pile of rubble. Abby raced inside, hurrying up the stairs, splinters snapping under her shoes.

The light returned, and Mina shortly followed, sending a wave of relief through Abby.

"It's clear," Mina said, her eyes bright with an intense curiosity. "No one's here. But I did find something."

"The binoculars?" Abby asked hopefully.

Mina shook her head. "A fork."

"Someone was eating up here?" Abby frowned. That seemed like a very odd and unsanitary thing to do.

"In the stairs," Mina elaborated. "They fork up ahead, come look."

Abby followed Mina up a few stairs, before realizing there was a suspicious lack of footsteps behind her. "Lucas?"

"I'll keep watch." Lucas peeked his head through the door. "The last thing we need is for the three of us to get trapped inside that place."

"Good thinking," Abby whispered back. She gave Lucas a thumbs-up, to which he replied by raising his thermos in what she presumed was supposed to mimic a toast but looked like an off-Broadway rendition of Oliver Twist begging for food.

Sighing, she turned back to Mina and followed her up the creaky stairs until they reached a small landing made of a wooden platform, which was surprisingly sturdy compared to the stairs. In fact, some of the wood panels looked like they had been recently replaced with crisp, pale stretches of wood. "Take a picture of this."

Mina raised an eyebrow. "The landing?"

"I want to know what Lucas thinks of the architecture," Abby explained. It would take way too long to convince him to come inside and see for himself. She could only hope a picture would be good enough.

Mina shook her head, unconvinced, but prepared to take a picture anyway. She raised her phone. "Smile. This place is too cramped to get anything without us in it. And besides, I've been wanting a selfie with you anyway."

Abby smiled and made a series of progressively funnier faces as Mina snapped a few pictures, both of them breaking into laughter on the sixth one. Mina's laughter was a warm, deep, melodic song that made Abby feel lighter and warmer by merely witnessing it. Abby found herself grinning as Mina turned her camera around, swiping through pictures for Abby's approval. Though the pictures caught Mina's radiant smile and Abby's windswept hair looked impressively glossy, there wasn't much of the wood paneling for Lucas to look at. Abby was about to suggest they take another when she noticed a glimmer behind Mina's right shoulder. She took the phone, pinching the screen to zoom in.

"What's that?" Mina asked as Abby zoomed so far in, the glimmer filled the entire screen in a burst of gold.

"I don't know." Abby returned the phone to Mina and turned around, surveying the floor in the general area where the shine had originated. Between two planks, something small and golden stuck out, barely the size of a hairpin.

Crouching, Abby plucked the thing from between the floor-boards. It slipped out without much resistance, though some beads came loose in the process, spilling over the floor in a sea of gold and black dots.

"It's an earring," Abby said, holding the hook in her thumb as she cradled the bottom with her palm to keep more beads from spilling. "A beaded earring."

"Huh." Mina crouched beside her. "What are you thinking?"

"I'm not sure yet," Abby admitted, pocketing the earring. It could have belonged to her attacker, just as easily as it could have belonged to someone who had passed through this place decades ago, when it could have been a harmless passage—a back entrance to someone's own bedroom. Abby wished she still had her walkie-talkie so she could ask Matilda and Violet about it. "Let's see where this passage goes."

"That one goes to Charles," Mina said, gesturing to the stairs that continued to climb to their left. "If I'd known you wanted to play around in this place, I wouldn't have helped David board it up last night."

"You wouldn't have let me stay last night if it hadn't been boarded up," Abby countered.

"True."

"And this door goes—where?" Abby asked, turning to her right, where the landing ended in an arch with yet another hidden door. This one had a clear handle, at least.

"There's one way to find out." Mina nodded toward the handle.

Abby raised a finger to her lips. As much as she didn't want to open a door into a room with an unsuspecting sleeping guest, she had to know where this door led. Cautiously, she pulled the handle and found herself face to face with what appeared to be the inside of an empty cabinet, with ropes hanging from either side.

"It's a dead end," Abby whispered, flinging the door open further and gesturing for Mina to look.

Mina's eyes widened. "That's not a dead end. It's a dumb-waiter."

"A what?"

"Something they used to send things up and down, from

room to room. Like an old-fashioned elevator for food and drinks."

"An elevator, huh?" Abby ran her finger along the dusty exterior. An elevator to where?

"Not for people," Mina stressed, accurately predicting where Abby's thoughts would take her next. It was small, but not too small for Abby. She could sit cross-legged comfortably inside.

"I could fit."

"It's dangerous." Mina's whisper grew harsh with concern. "The ropes could break."

"The ropes are clean, not even frayed," Abby said, examining the crisp, oddly white ropes. "This thing looks like it's been recently repaired and I want to know why."

Mina shook her head, her arms folded across her chest. After several seconds, she took a deep, wavery breath. "Fine. But, if you get stuck, or if you can't breathe, you punch the top of that thing as hard as you can, and then cover your head. I'll break the top open."

"You can do that?" Abby asked, once again impressed and slightly intimidated by Mina's many physical talents.

Mina's eyebrows pinched together. "I sure hope so."

Abby crawled into the dumbwaiter. The wood was solid, remarkably free of splinters and dust. She leaned against the back wall, crossing her legs in front of her.

"Move forward," Mina instructed. "Keep your hands in your lap, don't touch the rope or the walls."

"Thanks and I'll enjoy the ride," Abby replied, amused by how much Mina's instructions mimicked those of a theme park tour guide.

"I'm serious," Mina said, reaching for the ropes. "Give these ropes three tugs when you want to come back up."

As Mina pulled the ropes, Abby felt the ground lurch under her, and found herself gradually slipping lower and lower, like she was in a deflating ball pit. Soon, she was halfway behind a wall, looking up at Mina's gritty expression.

"Be careful," Mina reminded her, with a tender note of concern that made Abby's heart melt. "Let me know if you need out."

One more lurch and she was only able to see the toes of Mina's butterfly boots. Then, she was submerged in darkness. She shut her eyes. It was easier to tolerate the total darkness that way, when it felt like it was in her control. As the wood lurched under her and the ropes groaned, she imagined she was back in a childhood playground, playing hide and seek. Lucas would never have found her.

She hoped whoever had attacked her wouldn't find her either.

Had it really been Nathan? What did he want with her equipment? And if he had carried the candles upstairs, what had he planned to do with them before the ghost rearranged them? Or had he rearranged them into that chilling message? Was Nathan accusing a ghost of murder? Dozens of questions swirled in her brain, each of them stirring up more questions.

When several seconds passed without a lurching sensation, Abby risked opening her eyes. It was still dark, but not the total darkness that she had had when she was between the walls. While her view was obscured by a wall, a thin strand of light broke the center.

Abby reached out to the wall and pushed. It swung open easily—the side she had pushed, at least. She pushed the other side open and it swung out with a faint *creak*.

She blinked, adjusting to the faint glow of moonlight that

came through a far window, illuminating what appeared to be a large tomb. No, not a tomb—the kitchen.

Abby scrambled out of the dumbwaiter and onto a marble countertop that her mother would be envious of. The dumb-waiter groaned, rising an inch before lowering again, like the belly of a sleeping puppy. That was probably Mina, wanting to bring her back up. Abby jumped off the counter and opened drawer after drawer of cooking supplies, before finally finding one that had an open pack of pens. She grabbed a paper cup from the countertop and scribbled a quick note:

In kitchen. Come join me. There's coffee :)

After placing the cup in the dumbwaiter, Abby gave the ropes three sharp tugs and watched as the shelf slowly ascended. She turned back to the kitchen, ready to investigate. The problem was that she had no idea what to look for. Nathan wouldn't have fit in the dumbwaiter. Abby had barely fit, and he was at least a foot taller than her, and twice as broad-shouldered.

Abby rubbed her eyes. This was starting to feel like a dead end. Continuing to move through the kitchen, Abby opened drawers and cabinets, rummaging through their contents, hoping to find some clue that would jump out at her and make everything that had happened in the past few days make sense—or, against all odds, perhaps she would even stumble across her stolen equipment.

Abby was so invested in her search to find _something_ that she didn't even react when the lights turned on.

It wasn't until a voice called "Can I help you?" that she remembered she wasn't technically supposed to be here.

She turned to where Susan stood in the back doorway, strands of her blonde hair coming loose from her ponytail. Despite her scowl, she was still preferable to Nathan.

"I was just looking for coffee," Abby lied. "We're out. I didn't want to trouble anyone at this hour."

"Instant coffee is in here." Susan reached for a cabinet Abby had already checked. Abby noticed she was wearing her usual uniform and floral jewelry, but her red lipstick and dark mascara were smeared as if she had slept in it, and she wore a pair of fluffy bunny slippers. "Mugs are on the shelf by the sink."

"We already have those," Abby said, taking the instant coffee and backing toward the door.

"If you don't mind waiting, I can put on a real pot," Susan added, stifling a yawn. "Breakfast will start in an hour, but we have coffee and tea available before that."

At that moment, Mina and Lucas raced inside. Mina's fists were raised as if she was prepared to strike someone and Lucas had his phone out, ready to call for help.

"I got the coffee," Abby called, holding up the packets and hoping they would catch onto her cover story without making this more awkward.

Mina nodded, lowering her fists.

"Since when do you drink coffee?" Lucas asked, clearly confused.

"They're for me," Mina said, moving to Abby's side. She planted a kiss on Abby's cheek. "Thanks, love."

Abby couldn't tell if the term of affection was genuine, or another elaboration on their cover story, but her heart raced and she glowed under the affection.

"We got what we needed, thanks for your help," Abby called to Susan as she ushered her friends out of the kitchen and into the main dining room. She shut the double doors behind her, letting out a heavy sigh of relief.

"Find anything?" Mina whispered.

Abby shook her head, starting toward the main hall. As she moved through the dining room, lights flickered on, spilling a soft glow over lace tablecloths and decadent chairs. Except, it wasn't the overhead lights. In the large windows, string lights hung from floor to ceiling, carefully arranged so they clearly spelled out a message. Abby had to take a step back to see the entire thing. As she did, chills ran down her spine. It read: ***Happy Death Day.***

Lucas gulped. "The ghost?"

"Yes," Abby said, taking a cautious step forward. "Except, I don't think it's a ghost."

She followed the cord from the 'y' to where it disappeared through a small crack in the window. Opening the window wider, she gripped the cord and yanked until the lights went off. As she reeled in several more yards of cord, she turned back to the others. "I think someone is pretending to be a ghost."

Chapter Nineteen

"**W**hy would someone pretend to be a ghost?" Mina asked, lowering her voice so it would be lost in the gentle hiss of the radiator to anyone in another room.

"I haven't gotten that far yet," Abby admitted. "Who has been in the passage?"

"The two of us, David, and Sam," Mina replied.

"And whoever dropped this earring," Abby reminded her, lifting the broken jewelry from her pocket. "It's not really Sam's style. Didn't Dr. Greenwood have on gold jewelry yesterday?"

"Yes, but it wasn't beaded." Lucas rubbed the back of his neck. "And she didn't attack you, if that's what you're thinking. I was with her when I heard a crash, which must have been the binoculars falling."

"Susan wears a bunch of handmade jewelry," Mina pointed out.

"Yes!" Abby recalled the handmade sunflower earrings she had worn when Abby first arrived. The colors matched. "It must be Susan's!"

Lucas nodded, his expression calculating. "If I recall correctly, her lipstick matched the shade used to draw the message on the mirror. It's very red."

Mina tucked a strand of hair behind her ear, frowning. "But why would Susan attack you? And why on earth would she pretend to be a ghost?"

Lucas's eyebrows pinched together, a deep look of concentration on his face. "Oooh, ooh, I know!"

"You do?" Abby asked, impressed. "Is this something else they teach you in college?"

"Insurance money," Lucas said excitedly. "And no, I learned this from my day job. Sometimes, people destroy their own property for insurance money and then try to blame it on something else."

"Like ghosts?" Mina asked with an ounce of skepticism.

Lucas used two fingers to shove his glasses further up the bridge of his nose. "Usually, floods or an accident. But if this ghost rumor got big enough that it seriously hurt this place's reputation, then maybe that would count as an act of God."

"What does religion have to do with this?" Abby asked.

"Nothing," said Lucas. "That's just what the government calls things beyond your control, an act of God."

"And they say we have a separation of Church and Government," Abby grumbled.

"It's Church and State," Lucas corrected.

"Alright, so Susan—or someone—wants to make money off this place having a bad reputation?" Mina rubbed her temples.

"It's a theory," Lucas said. "Usually there has to be physical damage, not just financial."

A clattering of dishes rose from the kitchen, followed by a loud whirring noise.

"What about that maid that got hurt falling down the stairs?" Abby asked.

"Usually it's more like the roof got blown off so it's uninhabitable for a while."

Mina frowned. "The government would never buy that a ghost blew the roof off this place."

"They'd buy anything these days," Abby said with a shrug. "But so far, the ghosts have only made it more popular. Who would make more money if people keep coming here? Susan?"

Lucas shook his head. "Not if she's salaried. Nathan might, though. It depends on how much he puts into running the place, how much it costs to maintain. This counts as a historical building, so I imagine the fees are high—"

"It would explain why Nathan's so intent on getting us out of here," Abby speculated. "He could have stolen our equipment to make sure our story lines up perfectly with his. He must be paying Susan to go along with it. That's what we heard them arguing about. I thought she wanted to quit being a cook but what if she was actually thinking of backing out of whatever scheme they have to go after the insurance money?"

"Maybe." Lucas stroked his chin with his gloved hands, a strand of knitted yarn flaking off against his stubble. "He is getting a divorce, and those can be expensive. But he asked us to make the ghosts seem harmless. Wouldn't that go *against* this plan?"

"Not really. He wanted us to write about the ghost in a positive light so when the damage occurs, the ghost seems like a legitimate force to blame it on, but not something he could have predicted or prevented. He can say he didn't know any better and blame the ghosts."

Lucas looked stricken. "Or maybe he plans to blame it on *us*."

Abby gave Lucas a look that said she thought he was over-reacting, but then his theory began to make sense. What if Nathan planned to damage the house and leave *her* equipment behind to make it look like she'd been involved? It could work—for Nathan, which would mean bad news for her and Lucas.

"What about Sam?" Mina asked.

Abby turned to her. "What about them?"

Mina twisted her earring. "Aren't they the one that started this whole haunting rumor? If this place made national news, that could make their career. Can't you see the headlines? *Modern Marketing Protégé Transforms Failing Bed and Breakfast Into the Haunted Tourist Capital of the East Coast.*"

"It's not Sam," Abby said defensively.

Mina gave Abby a pitying look. "I know they're your cousin—"

"Whoever did this *attacked* me," Abby insisted. "Sam would never."

"No," Lucas agreed. "But Sam could be working with Nathan. Things might have gotten out of hand. Sam said they had it under control, but Nathan had a different idea."

Abby's insides knotted. The thought of Sam teaming up with someone like Nathan to frame Abby and Lucas was too outrageous. "They're not involved."

Mina looked as if she were about to argue, then shook her head. Moonlight winked off the silver buttons on her leather jacket as she paced the length of the garden windows. "So if we assume Nathan is the mastermind behind this, and that he really is planning on damaging this place for money and blaming it on the two of you—how do we stop it?"

"We need to figure out what his next steps are," Abby said.

"And we need to get one step ahead of him, *fast*."

"We can't exactly ask him," Lucas pointed out.

"No, but we can watch him. I know of the perfect spy."

IN THE PRE-DAWN glow, the world felt lighter. Trees began to stir, shaking frost from their limbs. Abby finished setting up the croquet course by the light of Lucas's phone, while he grumbled that she was killing his battery.

"You shouldn't have stayed up all night reading fanfiction," Abby countered.

"How was I supposed to sleep in a room surrounded by ghosts and robbers and who knows what else?" Lucas tucked his phone into his pocket.

"You seemed to be sleeping just fine when I tried to wake you this morning."

"That's because I got so exhausted around 1 a.m., my body couldn't handle it anymore. It can't handle *you* and your shenanigans anymore."

"All set." Abby dusted her hands as she stood from positioning the final hoop.

"I still don't understand how you expect this to work." Lucas poured a box of candy hearts into his palm and popped one into his mouth. "Without the walkie-talkie, Charles can't talk to us."

"No," Abby said. "But he can hear us, and that's all I need. For Charles to hear and acknowledge my words. Charles, if you are there, will you so kindly take a shot for me—"

Abby held out her croquet mallet. The morning air rustled her sleeve.

Mina and Lucas exchanged confused glances.

"Charles?" Abby asked. "Are you there?"

Seconds passed, with only the graze of the breeze against Abby's arm and the crunch of Lucas's munching filling the silence. Slowly, she began to lower her arm—but the mallet flew right out, pried from her fingers. It struck the ball, sending it directly through the first hoop and continuing to barrel down the lawn, rolling directly through the second hoop.

Lucas staggered back, spilling candy hearts onto the dirt. Mina's eyes widened.

Abby hollered in praise, before remembering she was supposed to be quiet. Slapping her hands over her mouth, she made a thumbs-up signal in the area of the mallet.

"He's here," she whispered triumphantly. "Okay, Charles, here's what I want you to do."

Abby could only hope that Charles was still around, able to hear her, and both motivated and strong enough to follow her requests. She spilled her suspicions about Nathan staging 'haunted activity' in order to scare people away as a plot to get insurance money. It sounded a bit far-fetched as she said it out loud, but Lucas filled in the details, making it sound more reasonable. She asked him to gather the other ghosts and trail Nathan, reporting back to her if they found anything.

"Without the walkie-talkie, we can't hear you," Abby stressed. "But I trust you'll get our attention if necessary. Will you help us with this?"

In response, a candy heart lifted from the ground. Abby held out her hand as it floated toward her open palm. When it landed, she flipped it over and saw a single word engraved in the candy. *Yes.*

Abby grinned. "Thank you."

"Wait a minute, I've got questions too." Lucas plucked the candy heart from Abby's hand and held it out in his palm. "Charles, did you know about the secret passageway?"

The candy heart lifted, then returned to his palm. "Yes."

Abby gave Lucas a quizzical look. What was he getting at? She didn't want him to tire out Charles, but she figured three questions couldn't hurt. She would give him that many, and then reassess.

"Was it there in your time?" Lucas asked.

The candy heart flipped over in his palm, revealing a blank side. Abby took that as a *no*.

"Okay, okay." Lucas bobbed his head in a manner that Abby had come to learn meant he was thinking deeply about something. "Did Nathan build it?"

The candy heart didn't move. Either the answer was no or Charles was no longer with them.

"I think that's enough questions," Abby said. "We don't want to tire him out."

"One more. Final question—I think I've got this." Lucas rolled his shoulders back and let out a deep breath as if he were playing one of those game shows on live TV. "Was the passage built during the Prohibition era?"

The candy heart flipped over. *Yes.*

Lucas whooped with joy. "I knew it!" He kissed the candy heart, then promptly dropped it—probably remembering it had been on the ground. He turned to Abby, grinning. "When I heard about that dumbwaiter, I thought for sure this was built during the Prohibition. People sure got crafty during those times. Turns out, alcohol is a good motivator."

"Okay, but this helps us—how?" Abby asked.

"It was definitely built before Nathan's time, but like I said, the siding is new. He must have found it, years ago, and chose to keep it open. And hidden." He dusted his palms, looking sadly at the candy hearts that remained face down in the dirt. "What do we do now?"

"We wait. And hope we aren't too late."

They returned to their room, where they packed, and ate a breakfast consisting of packaged snacks. The sky began to lighten as they carried their luggage to the car, and one by one, the windows began to light up as bleary-eyed guests fumbled out of bed.

Abby had planned to make a big show of checking out at the front desk, promptly at 8 a.m. The only problem was that no one was there. Abby poked her head into the dining room, where Harvey cleared a table while Susan refilled a middle-aged woman's glass of orange juice. Her makeup had been refreshed and her slippers were replaced with her usual kitten heels, but even a fresh coat of makeup couldn't hide her exhaustion. She yawned, glancing toward a back corner, where Nathan sat, shoveling toast into his mouth. He paused when he saw Abby and his eyes narrowed.

"What are you still doing here?" He shoved his seat back with a loud grating sound and started toward her. If he didn't want to make a scene, he was doing a terrible job. Everyone into the room was staring at him. Granted, there were only two other couples, Harvey, and Susan, but still—what little conversation had been occurring fell silent.

Nathan snatched Abby's arm, pulling her back into the hall.

"I'm just checking out," Abby said innocently, holding up her key. "No one was at the front desk."

Over Nathan's shoulder, the chatter in the breakfast room began to pick up. Clearly Abby's remark had been enough to make the guests dismiss Nathan's outburst as uninteresting. Susan alone kept her gaze on Abby, lips pressed in a disapproving frown.

"Where's Sam?" Nathan asked, before barking over his shoulder, "Sam!"

When Sam didn't magically come running in from the kitchen, Nathan sighed.

"Harry!" he snapped, turning his attention to Harvey.

It took the poor old man a moment to realize Nathan meant him.

By that time, Nathan was halfway through his spew of orders. "Please show this young lady and her friends to the door and ensure they do not come back. If you see them around again, call the police. They are not welcome here."

He waved a hand in Abby's direction as if attempting to shoo a fly away before turning back toward his table.

Harvey flinched, returned the dishes he had just picked up to the table, and turned toward Abby, joining her in the hall.

"Guess this is goodbye," Abby said.

"Guess so," Harvey replied, wiping his hands on his apron. "Where are your friends?"

"Packing up the car," Abby said. "Aren't you going to ask what I did to get that kind of treatment?"

Harvey raised an eyebrow. "Do I want to know?"

Abby sighed. "I just get the feeling he doesn't like me."

"Seems like it." Harvey held out his hand, which smelled strongly of dirt and cleaning chemicals. "How about I just take your keys and I'll email you the receipt?"

"Technically, you hired me, so I think you keep the receipt."

"Ah," said Harvey, looking utterly confused. He started toward the front office, wincing as Cupid's barking drifted in from the dining room. "Wait just a minute, then."

Abby followed him inside, scanning the room one final time for any clues that may shed light on Nathan's sinister intentions. She picked up the photograph on the desk, running her thumb along the golden frame. The Nathan who grinned back at her from behind the glass had fewer wrinkles and slightly darker hair, but the same overly-practiced smile. "So this place belongs to Nathan?"

"Yep." Harvey adjusted his glasses and leaned toward the computer, flexing his fingers before pressing the power button.

"Is he the sole owner of this place?"

"Yep." Harvey typed in a password. It was wrong.

"The caps lock is on, just so you know." Abby returned the frame to its previous position, moving deeper into the room. "And is he planning on selling it?"

"Dunno." He turned off the caps lock and tried typing the password again. This time, it worked.

"You wouldn't happen to know anything about the insurance policy on this place, would you?"

Before Harvey could answer, Nathan barged in. "What is she still doing here?"

"I'm getting her checked out," Harvey said. "She said—"

"I don't care what she said. Susan needs you in the kitchen."

"But—"

"No buts!" Nathan snapped. "That damn dog keeps trying to get into the pantry. Put him out back and then help Susan. And you—" He steered Abby toward the front door. "Have a wonderful rest of your day. Away from here."

Harvey sighed, muttering something under his breath that sounded suspiciously like "Only thing I can do in the kitchen is burn the place down."

Abby stopped in the doorway, turning back to face Nathan. She wasn't sure what made her do it, but something in Harvey's words reminded her of the fire. Perhaps Violet's death *had* been an accident, but Nathan's family had somehow profited from it. "Did your dad get insurance money from the fire?"

Nathan turned back to Abby, his eyes widening with a look of confusion, then anger. She took a cautious step back as he moved close to her, his jaw clenched.

"That fire nearly killed my family. It nearly killed *me*." He rubbed his temples, shaking his head. "This whole ghost thing was a mistake. It's time for you to go."

He shut the door in Abby's face. It closed with a gentle *click*.

In the seconds that followed, Abby's line of thinking stirred a horrid, dreadful idea—the only ghost Nathan had imitated was the ghost of Violet Lovelace. The girl who had died in a fire, almost fifty years ago, at a romantic Valentine's Day dinner—the very dinner they were recreating tonight. She recalled the message they had seen this morning and a lump formed in her throat. *Happy Death Day.*

Recreating the dinner was only step one of his twisted plan—he was going to recreate Violet's death. He was going to burn the bed and breakfast—maybe even with someone trapped inside.

Chapter Twenty

Abby was quite familiar with Lucas's expression of disbelief—the way his eyebrows narrowed into a quizzical look, his head tilted to the left, and his mouth soundlessly formed the word 'what?'

Abby was less familiar with Mina's tells, but judging from her rigid posture and downcast eyes, she wasn't buying Abby's theory.

"Why is it so hard to believe?" Abby asked, putting the car in park and turning around to face Mina in the backseat, her dark hair illuminated with the neon light of a fast-food restaurant in the adjacent parking lot.

Mina gave a slight shake of her head. "Aside from the fact that it's difficult to believe anyone would want to burn down their own building, it seems rather elaborate, don't you think?"

"And we don't have any proof." Lucas tugged at his seatbelt. Despite the car being in park, with the engine running only to keep the heat on, he seemed reluctant to take it off.

"But we do," Abby said. "The candles, the fogged glass, the lights—someone wrote those messages, trying to make it look like a ghost."

"How can you be sure?"

"Aside from how elaborate that message in the string lights was this morning, why would a ghost plug them in outside? Why not plug it in the room outlet? Unless you're worried someone would see you—in which case, you aren't a ghost."

"Maybe the ghost is afraid of whoever stole the binoculars."

"But before they even knew we were here, someone wrote that message on the bathroom mirror. How does a ghost write a message on a mirror? They would have to pick up a rag or something tangible, which the guests would have noticed— but a human could have easily slipped in before the guests arrived, wrote a message with their finger, and no one would have noticed until the steam came on. I used to do that to my parents all the time—leave funny messages for them to find the next time they took a shower."

"Wait, that was you?" Lucas cried. "You did that at my house too, didn't you?"

"Maybe?" Abby scratched the back of her head. "I think once or twice."

"You scared me to death. I didn't shower in my own bathroom for a year—I would only use my parents'."

"And the extra candles were carried through the secret passageway," Mina surmised, steering the conversation back on track.

Lucas shot a final disapproving glance at Abby before shaking his head. "But Nathan didn't arrive until *after* that message had been left in Violet, and someone painted over the Valentine's Day dinner sign."

Pine needles danced against the windshield as a gentle breeze hummed through the vacant parking lot. A faint floral scent filled the car, catching Abby's attention. Not far away, a radiant elderly woman set up a flower stand on the sidewalk, reminding the world it was Valentine's Day.

"We don't know that for sure, do we?" Abby pointed out. "He said his flight had been delayed, but did anyone check? He could have been staying anywhere—perhaps even in the secret passage."

Lucas adjusted his seatbelt. "I don't know. A guy like that, sleeping in a dusty stairwell, doesn't add up."

"He could have paid someone," Mina speculated.

"Like Susan," Abby agreed. "Maybe she wrote most of the messages while Nathan was out."

Lucas leaned forward. "Except the message written in her lipstick is the one written in Nathan's handwriting."

"Then that's proof they're working together," Abby said excitedly. "He must have been showing her what he wanted her to do."

"But how do we know he plans to burn the building down?" Lucas asked. "That's a pretty big leap from writing spooky messages."

"Not really. All the messages have been 'from' Violet—encouraging people to remember that she died on Valentine's Day, at this very dinner, forty-nine years ago. When Harvey went into the shed, I saw way too many cans of gasoline in there. Someone is stocking up. I'm pretty sure it's Nathan. He's planning on making 'Violet' burn down the building tonight, and then he's going to blame it on us, claiming *we* were the ones faking Violet's ghost."

Lucas nodded slowly. "In a weird way, that actually makes sense."

"It sounds complicated." Mina folded her arms across her chest. "I'm not saying you're wrong, Abby, but I'm not saying you're right either—if Nathan really is planning to burn down a building, we should go to the police."

"No," Abby and Lucas said at once.

"They'd never believe us," Abby said.

"They might even arrest us," Lucas added. "I don't know about you, but my plans for the next 120 days do *not* involve sitting in a jail cell for trespassing."

"Fine." Mina slumped deeper against the back seat. "What do you suggest, then?"

In the silence that followed, Abby realized both Lucas and Mina were looking at her for answers. She reasoned aloud, "Well, we can't let him burn down the place. But there's not much we can do without evidence. And we can't get caught. I say we wait a few hours and sneak back in when the guests arrive. That way, there will be more people to blend in with, and Nathan will hopefully be busy helping seat everyone. We can take the back door into the kitchen, hide in the pantry and…stop him if he comes in with a box of matches."

Lucas's eyebrows pinched together. "That sounds like a very dangerous plan."

"Do you have a better one?"

"Yeah. We go home and check the news tomorrow. If the place is burned, we send in our suspicions to Nathan's insurance company."

"But what if people get hurt? What if someone gets trapped inside like last time?"

Lucas pressed his lips together, folding his arms across his chest.

"Isn't your sister going to be there?" Mina asked.

He shook his head, reaching for his phone. "Not if I text her first."

"Can you text Sam too?"

"What's their number?"

Abby chewed her lip, realizing she didn't know. The only numbers she had memorized were her parents' and Lucas's. She could call her mom and ask, but she'd rather avoid that.

"Abby." Lucas's voice stiffened. "Why is my phone at five percent battery?"

"I didn't use it much," Abby insisted. "Just to look up a few things and listen to some music while we were packing."

"We had speakers in the hotel room—my phone was supposed to be charging."

Abby shrugged apologetically. "I forgot to plug it back in."

Lucas tightened his grip on his phone. "How are we supposed to get home without GPS? How am I supposed to warn my sister not to go to a dinner hosted by a potential arsonist? And if we do end up following your incredibly dangerous plan, how are we supposed to call for help if your phone's broken and mine's dead?"

"You can use mine," Mina offered.

Shaking his head, Lucas texted Michelle, then powered off his phone. "I'm saving what little battery I have left."

"We can get the ghosts to help," Abby added. "Maybe they can find our equipment. Or they could at least lock Nathan up somewhere until after dinner."

"Oh great, now we're putting our lives in the hands of ghosts."

"I like Abby's plan." Mina nodded affirmingly. "Let's take it easy until evening, and head back around sunset. We can figure out the details in the meantime."

"I can't say I like this." Lucas slumped back against the passenger seat as Abby switched the car into drive. He added thoughtfully, "If I save Dr. Greenwood's life, do you think she'll give me an interview?"

Chapter
Twenty-One

The garden looked majestic. Maybe it was the numerous orb lights that hung from branches, or the glass windows ablaze with orange sunset, or merely the fact that Abby studied it from a distance, peering between evergreen needles—but it looked larger, more magnificent than she remembered. Several couples sat on the back patio, sipping wine at romantic candle-lit tables between large heating lamps as the breeze playfully tickled their shawls and winter coats.

Music drifted through the garden, its faint melody reaching Abby's hiding spot.

"It's getting dark," Abby said, itching to move. In the past few hours, they'd revised their plan time and time again, even brainstorming a list of places Nathan could have stashed their equipment. The front office seemed the most likely place—but there was also his car, the room he'd been staying in, the shed, and the entire main house. Abby brushed her thumb over the list of potential hiding spots that she had tucked in her pocket.

Hopefully, she could get it to Charles.

"Not dark enough we can sneak across the yard unnoticed," Lucas replied.

Abby let out an exasperated sigh. Lucas was right, but that didn't do anything to appease her boredom.

"How about a game of twenty questions?" Lucas suggested, rolling up the sleeves of his sweater. "You guess first."

"Is that when someone thinks of a famous person and the others ask yes or no questions to try to guess who it is?" Mina asked. In her fitted sweater, denim skirt, and leggings, she looked charmingly romantic. She had clearly packed for a date, not a stakeout. If they stopped Nathan in time, maybe Abby could take Mina somewhere nice after.

"Yes." Lucas held up both hands and lowered his pinky finger. "Nineteen questions left."

Mina rolled her eyes. "Are you sure this is a good time to play games?"

"Yes." Lucas lowered another finger. "Eighteen questions."

"Are you human?" Abby asked, hoping a game would help her focus. She still wasn't entirely sure how to confront Nathan. Not without more evidence.

"Yes," Lucas replied, lowering another finger.

"Are you alive today?" Abby asked, wishing solving this case would be as easy as guessing Lucas's person.

Lucas shook his head. "No."

"Were you ever alive?" Abby pinched the bridge of her nose, wishing she could question Nathan instead. Why would he go through all this trouble to fake a ghost? And why recreate the fire? If he wanted insurance money, weren't there less elaborate ways to get it?

"Nope," Lucas said, sounding pleased with himself.

That meant his character was fictional. Abby proceeded to ask three more questions before correctly identifying Lucas's character as Elizabeth Bennet from *Pride and Prejudice*. After three more rounds, the sun sank below the horizon. Abby could barely make out the outline of her companions when they were three feet away.

She stood, her coat shedding pine needles. "I think it's time."

Mina nodded in agreement. As much as Abby didn't like the idea of splitting up, they had agreed it would be best for someone to remain outside, in case the others were caught. Lucas had enthusiastically volunteered.

Abby and Mina stepped out of the bushes as the roar of an engine grew louder. Abby turned to find a pair of headlights near the front of the house. They grew larger, moving toward her.

"I didn't know there was a road back here," Abby said, confused.

Mina pulled Abby back behind the bushes. "There isn't."

"What was that?" Lucas whispered, alert. "It sounded like a car."

"It is," Abby replied, as the engine grew louder, chugging a car directly across the back lawn, the headlights brightening their hiding spot. Abby tensed, preparing to run deeper into the woods. If Nathan was trying to run them over in his own backyard, he was more dangerous than she had thought.

Yards away, a car door opened and shut. Abby held her breath. Risking a glance over her shoulder, she peered under the needles to where someone in dark work boots got out of a black Mercedes-Benz. The headlights flared to life once more as the car beeped shut. It was Harvey who stood there—his features older and more sinister in the harsh flash. There was just enough illumination to see him tuck the keys into his pocket, and turn back toward the house. In the darkness that followed, the crunch of his footsteps grew slowly quieter, along with his muttering.

"Do you think he was looking for us?" Abby whispered.

"I think he's acting as valet," Mina replied, nodding toward the side parking lot that was clearly full, despite less than a dozen cars parked there. "Which means, we should go now before he parks another one."

Abby nodded, forcing herself to stand, against her instincts, which told her to remain hidden until Harvey was long out of sight. Brushing aside the branches, she emerged into the back garden. She started slowly forward, keeping her distance from the Mercedes, which loomed to her left, an inky shadow against the darkness.

Mina stepped out beside her and stopped, frowning. "Is that David's car?"

Abby turned to give the car a proper look. It was black, sleek, and had the Mercedes logo in too many places. "I have no idea."

Cupping her hands around her eyes, Mina moved toward the driver's window and peered in. "It is. Check out the car ornament hanging from the mirror. It's the one your mom gave them."

"My mom got them a car ornament?" Abby joined Mina, peering inside, to a very clean, very dark interior. The reflection of the garden light sparkled off the mirrors, revealing a small ornament with the words 'Happily Ever After,' followed by a date too small to read. Abby didn't need to make it out. The basset hound tumbler in the cup holder was a clear giveaway it belonged to David. That guy really loved dogs.

Abby shook her head. "My mom has bad taste. And Lucas is going to hate this."

"What am I going to hate?" Lucas asked.

Mina and Abby parted like he had caught them doing something scandalous.

Abby pointed at the car. "We're pretty sure this is David's car."

Lucas tilted his head as he considered the implications of that statement. His eyes narrowed. "I told Michelle not to come!"

He slipped his phone from his pocket. It flared with blue light as he powered it on.

Mina and Abby immediately covered the screen with their hands, ushering Lucas back into the bushes.

"We really need to go." Mina tilted her neck toward the house. "Who knows when Harvey will be back with another car."

"We need to get my sister out of there," Lucas insisted. He started to call Michelle, but his phone died on the second ring. He shoved it back in his pocket with a grunt of annoyance.

Abby put a reassuring hand on his shoulder. "We'll stop Nathan. Michelle will be fine."

Lucas tugged on his collar, shaking his head. "I'm going with you."

"But someone needs to stay here."

"I'll stay," Mina offered.

Abby turned to her, both admiring how quickly she could adapt to a new plan and sad that this meant they would now be separated. "Are you sure?"

"Yes." Mina reached out and gave Abby's hand a reassuring squeeze. "Now go—quickly. And be careful."

"You too," Abby whispered.

Lucas shoved aside the tree like it had personally harmed him and stomped across the garden.

With a final longing glance in Mina's direction, Abby tore off after him. She wasn't surprised when Lucas angled not toward the kitchen—as planned—but toward the back porch where the guests were seated. At least he had the good sense to duck behind a stone pillar, and not stroll in through the back door. Who knew where Nathan was, or who he had helping him?

"Lucas," Abby hissed, crouching down behind him. "The kitchen is that way."

"But my sister is that way." Lucas peered around the stone pillar at the guests on the back porch.

Abby nudged him. "Get up, you look like a creep."

"But people will see us."

"That's okay as long as we blend in. Stand straight and take my arm."

Abby stood, half dragging Lucas beside her. She pried his arm away from his side and slipped her arm through his before leading him onto a garden path, faking a loud giggle.

"Stop looking like you're scared to death," she whispered. "Pretend you're on a date."

Lucas gulped. "I *am* scared to death on dates."

Abby pulled him into a hug, resting her chin on the scruffy shoulder of his coat. From here, she had a good look at the tables. A woman, who looked particularly bored while on her date with a man who was checking his phone, glanced in her direction. She kept her expression locked in a fake smile as she scanned the couples, looking for Michelle and David.

"They aren't here," she declared, stepping away from Lucas.

"They must be inside."

Lucas turned toward the house.

Abby grabbed his hand, steering him back toward the garden. "There's no way we're getting in that house without Nathan or his staff seeing us. We need to wait until we see Sam. Or better yet, stick to the original plan."

"The plan that involved ghosts helping us out? How do you expect to contact Charles without your croquet set?"

Abby chewed her lip. She had been hoping the set would still be out, but now that it had clearly been moved to make room for the valet cars, she needed a new plan. "I'll think of something."

The wind picked up, chilling her nose and rattling the hedges. Behind her, metal creaked.

Lucas buttoned the top of his coat. "While you do that, I'm going to get my sister out of danger."

"Wait." Abby grabbed his arm, gesturing to the swing that swayed gently in the wind. "Violet."

Lucas's eyes widened. "Is she here?"

"Probably," Abby said, although she couldn't be sure. The wind was pretty strong. Could it have swayed the bench swing? Abby glanced at the purpling sky, where the sun had dipped below the horizon. Violet could just as easily be on that swing, watching the lingering sunset.

Slipping the paper from her pocket, Abby headed toward the bench. "Violet? Are you here?"

The bench continued to sway, creaking in the fading breeze.

After smoothing the paper between her thumb and index finger, Abby rested it gently on the armrest. "I hope you are. We could really use your help. We think Nathan plans to recreate the fire that killed you and burn down the bed and breakfast for insurance money. We're going to stop him."

The bench slowed until the swaying stopped altogether. Music continued to pour from the back porch, louder now that the wind had stopped.

"I don't think she's here," Lucas whispered in annoyance.

Abby shrugged. "We have to hope she is. Let's get to the kitchen."

"Michelle first," Lucas insisted, moving toward the patio.

"Please," Abby whispered to the empty bench and the ghost that hopefully occupied it. "Help us prove this man is up to no good before he endangers everyone tonight."

Abby took a final look at the swing before following, leaving her instructions behind. She really hoped Violet was there—and prepared to help—or the odds were stacked against them.

Jogging to catch up with Lucas, she followed him onto the patio and toward the back door. When he reached it, instead of going inside, he leaned his hands against the window, peering in.

Abby elbowed him. "Subtle, remember."

"I can't believe this!" Lucas cried, loud enough to attract attention from two nearby tables.

"What?" Abby asked, giving up all pretense of trying to act like they belonged. "Do you see your sister?"

"Dr. Greenwood's having dinner with Jeffery."

"Jeffery." Abby scrunched up her nose. "The carriage guy?"

"Yes, the carriage guy, who works for the Inn." Lucas grabbed the roots of his short hair. "You know, the one that Michelle and David stayed at last night? That Sam was so concerned about. What if Sam was right all along?"

"I thought you said Dr. Greenwood wasn't involved in this."

"I said she couldn't have attacked you. I was with her

when you went in that passage. But if she was working with Jeffery—"

"Then Jeffery could have attacked me." Abby tried to make sense of this new information. "But what possible reason could he have for wanting to fake hauntings?"

Lucas's eyes widened. "Dr. Greenwood said she's working on a book about this place. About *Violet*."

Abby gave him an unimpressed look. "And you didn't think to mention this before now?"

"I didn't think it was relevant."

"Well, it definitely seems—"

Abby didn't bother finishing her sentence as Lucas stormed inside, directly toward the table where Dr. Greenwood sat.

Abby sucked in a breath before dashing in after him. So much for going in with a plan.

It took Abby a moment to adjust to the dim candlelight and heavily scented air as various perfumes and colognes mingled with red wines and elaborate floral arrangements. When she had, she noticed Lucas standing beside Dr. Greenwood's table.

"Excuse me," Lucas said, using his over-pronounced polite tone that he usually reserved for the elderly and women he had a crush on.

"I think we need a few more minutes," Jeffery said, without looking up from the menu, clearly assuming he was a waiter.

Dr. Greenwood's eyes flared with recognition. "Lucas! Jeffery, this is Lucas and his friend, um—"

"Abby," Abby supplied.

"Abby!" She snapped her fingers as if she had just thought of it. "They're ghost hunters."

Jeffery turned to look then, and his face broke into a smile. He pointed his finger between Abby and Lucas. "You're the ones who ordered that ghost tour."

"Yes," Lucas said. "Unfortunately, our equipment got stolen last night. You wouldn't happen to know anything about that, would you?"

Jeffery tilted his head to the side as if he was genuinely attempting to understand the question.

"Who would do such a thing?" Dr. Greenwood asked. Her relaxed posture gave no indication she had anything to hide.

Lucas held up his finger and took a step back, angling away from the table as he whispered to Abby, "You think it was them?"

Abby shook her head. They were wasting time chasing a false lead, which she could have told Lucas if she had had more time to think.

"So, did I just accuse my dream boss of stealing?" Lucas's voice rose an octave.

"Not if you walk away now."

Lucas nodded. He turned back to Dr. Greenwood with a forced smile. "I hope you enjoy your dinner."

He slowly backed away, then turned and abruptly headed for the kitchen. Abby waved an awkward goodbye before following him.

Across the room, she noticed a couple seated at a table in a small, cushioned nook. They leaned toward each other, locked in an intimate embrace, a plate of cheese and crackers between them. A large diamond sparkled from the woman's ring finger. A familiar-looking diamond.

"I think I see your sister," Abby said, at the same time as Michelle and David finished their kiss.

Lucas stormed toward them like a parent who had caught a kid out after curfew. "What are you doing here?"

"Lucas." Michelle dabbed her lips with a lace napkin. Candlelight sparkled off the beaded neckline of her red dress, making her look extra sophisticated and reminding Abby that her oversized flannel and jeans were *very* out of place. "Always a pleasure to see you."

"You want to try to get a table near us?" David asked, as friendly as ever, rolling up the sleeves of his button-down shirt. Somehow, the guy made wearing a suit look casual. He clearly wore them often. And this one must have been tailor-made, for it matched Michelle's dress perfectly.

Lucas inched toward Michelle. "Didn't you get my text? The one that said, 'Don't come to dinner—it's dangerous.'"

Michelle reached for her glass of wine. "Yes, I texted back. You never replied."

"My phone was off."

"Whose problem is that?"

"Abby's."

Abby flashed Lucas a look of betrayal. "Dude."

"What? You're the one who drained all my power."

"We tried to make reservations somewhere else, but everywhere was booked," David chimed in, reaching for a piece of cheese.

Abby doubted they had tried *everywhere*. She was pretty sure the fast-food restaurants would be open, but she doubted David had ever eaten fast food. She wondered if he even knew of their existence. He *must*, right?

"We had to put down a deposit for these reservations," Michelle added, returning her glass to the table and absently twisting a silver napkin ring between her sleek fingers. "They weren't included in the gift card, you know."

In the hall to their left, the bell to the front door clanked as someone stepped inside. Abby's heart pounded as she recognized Nathan.

Lucas's eyebrows were pinched so close together he looked like he was posing for a caricature artist. "I can't believe this. I—"

Abby grabbed his shoulder. "We have to go. *Now.*" She glanced at Michelle and David with a ferocity that she hoped conveyed the importance and sincerity of her words. "Don't tell anyone you saw us."

"But—" Lucas protested.

Abby tightened her grip, pulling him back into the main dining room and through the double doors into the kitchen.

The air instantly jumped from a cozy romantic warmth to unbearably hot as the tantalizing scent of seafood bisque bombarded Abby's senses. Relaxing music was replaced with machines whirring and liquids boiling. Four large pots bubbled on the stove over an oven that glowed with warmth between counters lined with trays of appetizers from smoked fish to mini quiches.

"I was talking to my sister," Lucas protested, rolling up the sleeves of his sweater.

"You were about to get arrested," Abby countered, picking up a deviled egg and popping it into her mouth. It was pleasantly spiced and satisfyingly creamy. "Nathan was heading straight toward us."

Lucas smacked his lips together and made a sound of disapproval. "That food is not for you."

"Oh come on, this is like a five-course meal, no one is going to starve because they're missing one—"

The double doors to the kitchen flew open. Lucas dropped to the floor, ducking under the kitchen counter, while Abby hurried to the pantry. She had just enough time to slip inside, but not enough to close it, before Susan entered the kitchen, a stack of dirty dishes in one hand. She hurried to the sink—which was thankfully on the other side of the counter that Lucas was hiding behind—and dropped them in with a *clank*. Straightening her apron, she moved to the stove, where she reached for a large ladle.

Through the slight opening in the pantry door, Abby met Lucas's gaze. She gestured for him to come toward her, while Susan's back was turned, otherwise she would stumble directly across him on her way back to the living room. He glanced from Abby to Susan, then back.

He was taking too long. One more scoop and Susan would be finished filling the bowl, heading back toward the dining room, walking directly past Lucas—

The double doors squeaked, then slammed, signaling someone else had entered the kitchen. Lucas pressed his back further against the counter as if hoping he could melt into it.

"How's it going?" Nathan's voice raised the hair on the back of Abby's neck, even before he stepped into her line of sight.

He headed straight toward Susan, circling around the opposite side of the counter, taking his time with every step. There was no way both of those people would make it out of the room without seeing Lucas, unless he moved from his hiding spot. She made a face, insisting that he *move*.

"Where?" he mouthed.

"Anywhere!" Abby mouthed back with a shooing motion.

"Busy," Susan said. "We're short-staffed. Table seven is still waiting on their champagne. And oh—where is Harvey? He was supposed to bring this steak to fourteen."

"I've put him on valet duty," Nathan said, inching closer to

Susan. He put his arm on her waist in a way that probably violated an HR code. "I promise I'll make it up to you."

"You better," Susan replied, leaning so close her beaded rose earrings brushed against the shoulder of his jacket.

He pressed his lips against hers in a way that *definitely* violated HR code.

From the counter, Lucas mouthed, "What's happening?"

Abby attempted to mimic kissing the back of her hand. Lucas scrunched up his nose in a signal that meant either he had no idea what Abby was mimicking or he knew exactly what she was mimicking and was disgusted by it. Didn't Nathan have a *wife?*

Susan broke the kiss, licking her lips as she turned back to the soup. She was glowing—and not just with happiness. The overhead light winked off a diamond on her finger. Since when had she worn an engagement ring? That definitely hadn't been there when Abby had first seen her, or even that morning, when she had shown up in bunny slippers, finding Abby snooping in her kitchen.

"The chef's still not back?"

"No," Susan moaned. "It's been half an hour! He said he just needed ten minutes."

"I'll go look for him," Nathan said, heading toward the left side of the kitchen, where a large steak rested on a plate beside a helping of mashed potatoes. It was on the same side of the kitchen as Lucas, several feet away from him. "That steak goes to fourteen, right?"

Abby gestured frantically to Lucas to move. He seemed to understand a second too late. As Nathan's footsteps rounded the back corner, Lucas crawled around the front, where he held his knees to his chest and looked like he was trying to breathe as little as possible.

Thankfully, Nathan didn't seem to notice. He was too preoc-cupied glancing back at Susan and whistling at her, in a way that no girl Abby had ever met before found attractive. But Susan actually smiled at it. Carefully balancing a tray of soup and wine, she whispered something in his ear that made him grin. Then she headed across the kitchen and into the dining room, the double doors swinging shut behind her.

Nathan shook himself, collected the plate of steak, and hurried out the door, humming softly. The second the doors swayed shut, Lucas crawled out from the opposite side of the counter to the pantry, and shut the door behind himself, gently shoving Abby deeper inside.

Her elbow knocked into a jar of pickles and sent it jutting dangerously close to the edge of the shelf. She steadied it as Lucas's panting slowed.

"That was close," Lucas managed to squeak out at last.

Abby nodded in agreement. It was too close.

Lucas wrung his hands. "I thought he was going to set the island on fire, burning me up first thing. Maybe he'd even use my shirt to strike the match."

"I don't think your shirt would make for good striking material," Abby said, leaning against shelves full of oversized baking supplies. Speckles of flour and powdered sugar tickled her nose, making her want to sneeze. She let it happen.

Lucas covered her mouth with his hand as if she had screamed.

Abby shoved him aside, whispering. "Relax, we're alone."

Thump.

Lucas whipped his head to the side, looking toward the back of the pantry. "Did you hear that?"

Abby considered the numerous guests dining on the other side of the wall and waved her hand dismissively. "Someone probably just accidentally kicked the wall."

Thump.

"Maybe," Lucas said warily. "Or maybe it's Nathan dragging a box of firewood toward us. We've got to get out of here before he uses us as kindling."

"About that." Abby cleared her throat. "I don't think he's planning anything."

The flour speckling Lucas's eyelashes made his blinking all the more dramatic. "What?"

"I mean, I could see him planning a romantic dinner with a side of divorce papers, but other than that—he didn't seem like a guy planning to burn down a building."

"Oh he didn't *seem* like it? Tell me, how does someone who is about to burn down a building 'seem'?"

"Angry, stressed, emotional—maybe even cold and calculating. Not the way Nathan seemed—self-assured, happy, cocky even."

"Maybe because his nefarious plan was all going according to plan?"

"Maybe," Abby admitted, but it wasn't adding up. She had been so convinced Nathan had been faking the hauntings for insurance money, that all the clues had seemed to fit into place. Until they didn't. That earring had belonged to Susan, which meant she had been in the passageway. She had thought she had been helping Nathan with his insurance scheme, but now it seemed more likely she was using it to sneak around with him before his divorce had been finalized.

"But you were so sure," Lucas said.

"I wasn't *sure*. I suspected," Abby clarified, shaking her head.

"Maybe he had a change of heart."

"Or maybe, he was never planning anything bad at all and we're trespassing here for no reason," Lucas's whisper rose with heated anger. "Did it ever occur to you that maybe you overcomplicated this? Maybe he wanted a good ghost story to stir up business—just like he said in his note to Sam—and nothing more."

Thump.

Abby frowned. "Then why did he attack me in the passageway?"

"I don't know. Maybe you walked in on him and Susan in an intimate moment and he panicked."

Thump. Thump.

"Maybe," Abby said. That attack in the passageway had felt premeditated, not like the instinctual reaction of someone caught in the middle of a passionate act. They'd used chemicals on her; that took time to prepare. It wasn't like Nathan could have whipped that out of his pocket mid-kiss.

Thump. Thump. Thump.

"Okay, that definitely came from in here." Lucas turned toward the sound and nudged Abby's foot. "Go check it out."

"Why don't you go?" Abby asked, suddenly becoming a bit fearful of crawling deeper into the dark to look for the origin of a mysterious thumping sound.

"Because you're the one who took this job," Lucas reminded her. "Now, go do it."

"Rock-paper-scissors?" Abby suggested.

Just as it looked like Lucas was considering this request, the kitchen doors slammed open. The thumping ceased. Lucas scooted to Abby's side, as far from the door as possible, holding a finger to his lips. Above the distant music, and faint humming of kitchen equipment, Abby could barely make out the sound of shoes squeaking across the polished floor. Men's cologne followed by a strong chemical scent wafted under the door as they passed.

She tried to tune it out as she re-examined everything she had learned this weekend. If Nathan wasn't the one behind the hauntings, that meant someone else was. Someone else who had access to all the rooms, who knew about the cameras and the secret passageway, was making it look like the bed and breakfast was haunted. And not just by any ghost—they were faking a haunting *specifically* by Violet, warning them not to go through with the Valentine's Day dinner.

Someone like—

"Harvey," Abby whispered, her eyes widening. Harvey had access to the shed. He could have been storing the gasoline in there. He knew about the previous fire and Violet's death. It was possible he knew about the passage as well. But what motive did he have?

Lucas gave her a confused look, before sniffing the air. "Does it smell like gasoline to you?"

Gasoline was exactly what it smelled like. Tiptoeing across the pantry, she hurried to a crouch by the door. The scent grew stronger. A colorless liquid trickled under the door. Abby touched it with her pointer finger and planned to bring it to her nose to sniff, but the second it touched her skin she knew what it was. Lighter fluid. Or kerosene. Something flammable.

She had been right. Someone was preparing to burn this place down, recreating the fire that killed Violet fifty years ago.

She had just been wrong about it being Nathan.

Pulling open the door to the pantry, Abby stepped into the kitchen. Her sneakers squeaked against the oily substance that now pooled across the floor. Behind the island, a man stooped, pouring a large can of gasoline.

"Harvey," Abby said coldly.

Harvey glanced up at her, continuing to empty the can onto the floor.

"You're going to set the kitchen on fire," Abby stated, surprising herself with the calmness of her tone, despite her eyes flickering to the double doors, which were now sealed shut with duct tape. "Why?"

After letting the last few drops fall to the kitchen island, Harvey tossed the empty can aside and reached for another. His wrinkled fingers slowly undid the lid, as he gave Abby an incredulous look. "If you could really talk to those ghosts, you'd know why."

"I could until you stole my equipment," Abby countered.

"You said you talked to her!" Harvey cried, his voice rising in anger. As he turned, Abby noticed a walkie-talkie clipped to the side of his belt. Not any walkie-talkie, *her* walkie-talkie, with its brass antique antenna amplifier.

"Violet," Abby whispered, as everything clicked into place. "You're the fiancé."

Chapter
Twenty-Two

A bby's excitement at getting the answers she had spent so long searching for was tempered by the sizzling soup that threatened to boil over at any moment. Abby wasn't sure if chunks of boiling seafood were enough to start a fire, but she wasn't about to take her chances.

She inched toward Harvey, holding up her palms to show she held no hidden weapon. "You were here that night. The night of the fire in 1975. You said you weren't, but you were, weren't you?"

"Of course I was," Harvey cried, sloshing a fresh can of gasoline across the counters, ruining the appetizers. Abby winced as it seeped over the wonderful deviled eggs. What a waste.

"So help me understand what you're doing here now?"

"This place deserves to burn."

"I got that." Abby raced to think of a way to reason with him, but she was missing too many pieces and her mind was

still trying to match the image of the weary old man she had
known the past few days with this cold-blooded killer. It didn't
make sense. He wouldn't gain anything if the place burned.
"Why? Did you start the fire fifty years ago too? Did *you* kill
Violet?"

"Hell no!" Harvey shouted, his fist flying toward Abby.

She covered her face, but he merely shook his fist.

"I tried to *rescue* her. She was in here, but the doors—" He
pointed to the double doors, leading into the dining room.
"They weren't like that. They locked. Mr. Wentworth—
Nathan's father—saw the fire and tried to contain it. He says he
didn't know Violet was in here, but I told him. I was screaming
at him the whole time. When the firefighters got here, I told
them to get Violet, but Mr. Wentworth sent them upstairs to
get his precious son. Guess which of us they listened to."

Abby shifted her weight. The answer was obvious, as Nathan
was alive and Violet clearly wasn't. "Why didn't you say any
of this before?"

"Nathan would have fired me, or sent me to jail! And he'd
keep on profiting off my Violet's death."

"I'm sorry that happened. I truly am," Abby insisted, trying
to calm him down. "But burning this place isn't going to bring
Violet back."

"I know that," he snapped. "I'm not like you, pretending I
can talk to the dead, scamming people with false hope."

Abby wanted to tell him that it wasn't a scam, that she could
truly talk to ghosts, but she didn't think it was a good idea to
argue with a man pouring gasoline right and left. Instead, she
tried to keep her voice calm as she asked, "Then why?"

Harvey sloshed another wave of gasoline against the
counter, splattering it dangerously close to the stove. "This
place deserves to burn. For what it did to Violet. To me."

"And what about the people in there?" Abby pointed a trembling finger toward the dining room.

"The Wentworths are *murderers*," Harvey insisted, tightening his grip on the can until his knuckles grew white. "They deserve to die. Just like she did."

"What about everyone else?" Abby asked, desperate to talk reason into him. If he stopped now, they could evacuate the building and no one would get hurt.

"I tried to warn them," Harvey said. "If they cared about Violet, they'd have stayed away. No decent person celebrates the anniversary of a stranger's death like it's some kind of holiday."

"I don't think they're celebrating Violet's death," Lucas said, peeking his head out of the pantry. Abby turned and found him staring directly at her, making an odd gesture at his belt like he wanted Abby to pull down her jeans. That couldn't be right.

"I think they're celebrating a holiday," Lucas continued, each word coming slow and stilted as he made a 'hurry up' motion to Abby, then pointed at Harvey. "It's called Valentine's Day."

Abby turned to Harvey, wondering what Lucas could possibly have meant. She couldn't see how taking the man's pants off could help. Maybe his belt had matches or a lighter? She saw the walkie-talkie clipped on his side, and it suddenly made sense. That must be what Lucas was asking about.

But what good would talking to ghosts do now? She couldn't think of a way they could help.

Except Violet.

Abby pointed at the walkie-talkie. "Were you able to talk to Violet?"

"This thing is a fake!" Harvey cried, prying the device from his belt and tossing it to the floor. It slammed against the tile, skidding toward Abby's feet and landing in a puddle of fuel. She snatched it, gently wiping the hem of her flannel along the speaker to remove the gas as she checked for damage. A small dent winked back at her from the side of the walkie-talkie, but the antenna appeared intact.

"It's not," she insisted, turning it on. "I swear. I've lost someone too. And I would give *anything* to talk to her again, just once. I can help you talk to Violet."

"I can talk to her when I'm dead," Harvey declared, tossing the remaining can of gasoline toward the stove.

Flames shot up, bursting in loud snaps and pops, clawing their way toward the ceiling. Abby raced toward the double doors and attempted to pry them open. Lucas was instantly at her side.

"They're here," he cried.

"I know," Abby replied, as reassuring as possible as she shoved her shoulder against the door. At the moment, she was more concerned about getting themselves out than Michelle and David. "They're smart. They'll be okay."

Lucas shook his head. "The ghosts. They're here. They gave me these."

Abby glanced down and saw the brass binoculars gleaming in Lucas's palm. If only he had shown her this thirty seconds ago, they may have been able to calm Harvey down *before* he set the building on fire.

Smoke poured toward Abby, evoking painful coughs. Lucas intensified his efforts, pressing his shoulder harder against the door and tearing a large chunk of tape. Abby sprinted to the block of knives, prying one before the flames could devour them. The metal was already hot, though not hot enough to burn her as she rushed back to the door. Flames followed the trail of fuel across the kitchen island, shattering glasses and cracking porcelain dishes in their wake.

"Harvey." Violet's voice crackled through the walkie-talkie. "What have you done?"

Relief surged through Abby. Violet was here. If anyone could calm Harvey, she could.

In the center of the kitchen, inches from the flames, Harvey stiffened. "Violet?"

Something tugged on the knife. Abby loosened her grip and it slipped from her hands, hovering in the air. She held her hands up cautiously and took a step back. "Lucas," she whispered, nodding toward the knife.

Lucas stepped away from the door as the knife drifted toward it. The blade slammed into the lock, splintering the side of the door. The knife reared back and thrust again.

On the third strike, the doors burst open. Smoke soared into the dining room. Lucas staggered onto the carpet behind it, gulping for fresh air.

Shouts broke out, followed by dozens of footsteps and cries of panic. Within seconds, a fire alarm began to blare.

Abby turned back to Harvey, who was staring at the flames, mesmerized. Extending the binoculars toward him, she took a hesitant step deeper into the kitchen. "Violet's here. Do you want to see her?"

Harvey made no indication he heard her, continuing to stare at the flames.

Abby glanced over her shoulder. Most of the tables were already clear as guests rushed outside in a panic. Michelle and David stood several feet ahead, supporting a coughing Lucas between them.

"Go," Abby insisted, gesturing toward the front door. "I'm right behind you."

As they turned to leave, Abby turned back to Harvey. He was barely three feet from the edge of the flames, smoke billowing around him.

From the center of the flames, the ghostly shape of a woman emerged. Violet. Even without using the binoculars, Abby could vaguely make out her red uniform, the waves of her blonde hair as she circled him.

"What the hell—?"

Abby turned to the voice behind her and noticed Nathan, frozen in the dining room, staring at Violet like he had— well, seen a ghost.

He shook himself, rounding on Abby. "I said nothing dangerous!"

Abby backed away, holding her hands over her head. "I had nothing to do with this."

"Violet." Harvey's voice cracked. "Is it really you?"

Nathan took a forceful step toward Abby, but his gaze drifted to Violet and his muscles relaxed.

Together, Abby and Nathan watched as Violet brushed a ghostly hand against Harvey's cheek. "It's me."

Harvey leaned into her, a sad grin spreading across his face.

"What are you doing, Harry?" Violet asked. "Why did you come back?"

"For you," Harvey insisted. "I knew—I hoped—that one day I'd see you again."

"I hoped so too." Violet's misty face broke into a sad smile as her voice crackled through the walkie-talkie in Abby's hands. "But not like this. I'd hoped you'd have moved on. Been happy."

Harvey stroked the mist. "How could I be happy without you?"

"How could you put such a weight on me?" Violet asked with a sigh. "I'm dead, Harvey. I have been for decades. Let me go. And all this time, I've been trying to figure out what's keeping me here. I now realize—it's you. I can't move on because you won't let me."

Her voice grew angry, her figure solidifying beside Harvey. Flames raged behind them, smoke coiling around their shoulders. Susan's cheerful embroidery soon darkened and turned to ash. Abby knew she should be running for the door, but she was too enthralled by the scene unraveling before her.

"I love you," Harvey confessed.

"The man I loved would never set a building on fire, or lock people in the shed."

The weight of her words triggered something in Abby's mind. No one had seen Sam all day. That wasn't like her cousin, especially when this was Sam's marketing event of the season. She turned toward Nathan in a panic. "Sam! He's locked Sam in the shed."

Nathan nodded, rushing out of the kitchen and toward the front door.

"No," Harvey grumbled, once Nathan was out of earshot. "The chef is in there. He caught me moving gasoline in through the back door."

He turned back to Violet, his eyes gleaming with tears. "I panicked. I didn't hurt him! Just tied him up."

Abby glanced out the back window, to the shed across the yard. At least he was far enough from the flames. "What about Sam?"

Harvey's face twisted into anger. He glared at Abby. "Sam

deserves to die! They made a mockery out of Violet—out of *you*." His voice hitched as he turned back to Violet.

That meant he *did* have Sam somewhere—somewhere close, where the fire would reach quickly. She remembered the strange thumping in the pantry, and how Cupid had been barking at it that very morning.

Abby charged forward, dropping to her knees as another burst of coughs consumed her. Smoke filled her vision, broken only by dangerously close flames.

"Goodbye, Harvey." Violet's voice strained as her figure grew soft, the edges blurring into pale white light, which spread through her as she faded.

"No!" Harvey shouted, snatching at the air. "Violet come back, Violet—"

He started toward the flames. Abby reached out and grabbed his legs, sending him to the ground.

"You'll die," Abby insisted.

Harvey shut his eyes as a fit of coughing struck him. "At least I'll be with her again."

"Dude, you have *got* to get over her." Abby scrambled past him to get to the pantry. She slipped her flannel off and wrapped it around her hand, reaching for the pantry's metal handle. Even through the fabric, it was unbearably hot.

She tugged open the door and the cool smoke-free air washed over her, a wave of relief. She knew it would be momentary, so she scrambled to her feet and rushed to the far end of the pantry, where a long wooden box lay against the far wall. It was the only place big enough for a human. Several boxes lay on top. Abby shoved them aside, ignoring the mess of broken bottles and spilled condiments. She flicked the latch and the lid burst open. Sam shot upright, muttering something obscured by a piece of cloth across their lips. Their eyes widened at the flames.

Abby helped Sam out of the box and ran back to the kitchen, dropping again to her knees as she crawled to the dining room. The flames coated almost everything now—including the ceiling. Sam's jewelry clinked as they hurried alongside Abby. They raised a finger, flicking off Harvey as they passed. He was sitting motionless, waiting for the flames to consume him. Abby caught his foot once more, and dragged him behind her, toward the safety of the living room.

This time, he did not protest. He seemed resigned, letting her guide him across the hot tiles to the carpeted dining room.

Nathan returned, a makeshift mask tied around his nose and mouth. He rushed to Sam's side. "Can you walk?"

It was a pointless question, considering Sam was crawling swiftly under the smoke, toward the front door.

Sam nodded. Nathan dropped to their side, slipping a pocket knife from his pocket. "Let me get that off you so you can breathe."

"Harvey." Abby coughed, unable to pull the old man much further as smoke filled her lungs and her muscles grew weak.

Nathan sliced the cloth from Sam's mouth, which resulted in a slew of loud guttural coughs. He patted Sam twice on the back, glanced toward Abby, and nodded. "I'll get him."

He crawled past Abby and reached for the old man's shoulder. Harvey's protests broke into a fit of coughs as Nathan grabbed him by both arms and dragged him into the main hall. Abby followed, standing when the air grew fresher. Sam remained on their hands and knees, crawling toward the front door.

"How long were you in there?" Abby asked, feeling a jolt of guilt that she hadn't checked on her cousin sooner.

"Since eight." Sam grunted, then coughed. "I'm actually enjoying this heat. That pantry is cold."

A large stone held open the front door. Abby hurried toward it; the cool night air was a more treasured relief than any prize offered in the 5K races her mom used to sign up for. She hurried down the front steps and collapsed onto the grass, taking deep, heaving breaths. A cup of water floated toward her—courtesy of a resident ghost, no doubt.

Abby gulped it down.

"Careful." Charles's voice came through the walkie-talkie. "Don't choke. This place is a little crowded. We aren't looking for any more ghosts at the moment."

"Although I doubt we'll be seeing much of Violet anymore." Matilda's usually stern voice oozed amusement. "She seems to have moved on."

"Wish we could say the same about old Harvey, eh?" Charles mused. "Poor man wasted his whole life on a dead girl."

Abby winced at his choice of words. It was true; Harvey was unhealthily obsessed with Violet. But it's not like letting go of the dead is easy. Abby knew that struggle too well. She hated to admit it, but deep down, she understood Harvey's pain and the wrongness he felt at Violet's death.

She glanced to where Harvey sat on the grass, a vacant expression on his face. Nathan stood behind him, keeping a firm hand on his shoulder. Susan wrapped her arms around Nathan, sobbing into his shoulder as he attempted to soothe her with one hand. Sam hobbled over, replacing Nathan's grip on Harvey so he could focus solely on Susan, who stopped crying long enough to give Nathan a passionate kiss and then promptly burst into another round of tears.

"Abby!" Mina hurried to her side, her strong arms wrapping

around Abby's shoulders, pulling her into a hug.

The wail of a firetruck sounded in the distance. Red and white lights glared from the street.

Mina kissed Abby's cheek, ignoring the layers of sweat and grime that Abby could feel making her skin break out. She reached up and wrapped her arms around Mina, burying her face in Mina's sweater.

"You're okay, you're okay," Mina repeated in a reassuring tone, as she rocked gently back and forth. Abby wasn't sure if she was the one Mina was trying to reassure, or if Mina was reassuring herself—either way, Abby wasn't going to complain. She simply savored the scent of Mina's skin, the way the firelight gleamed off her dark hair.

"I'm sorry I ever questioned Sam," Mina whispered.

"It's okay," Abby said, glancing toward her cousin, who was busy being bombarded by Cupid's enthusiastic face-licks. "I suspected the wrong people too. I can't believe I didn't even consider Harvey until the last minute."

"Well, Nathan was acting suspicious. And we *did* find Susan's earring in that passageway."

Abby had a strong suspicion that they had been using the passage for entirely different reasons. "Didn't Sam say Nathan usually stayed in Charles?"

Mina nodded, her gaze drifting to Nathan and Susan's passionate embrace. "Wait—you don't think they used that passage to hook up?"

"Among other things. It does go to the kitchen after all. I think that message, the one written in red lipstick, wasn't part of the fake hauntings at all. Lucas was right—Nathan wrote it, with Susan's lipstick, but I don't think he meant anything creepy by it. I think he meant 'ready to join me?' in a sexy way, but with everything else going on, someone else saw it and interpreted it differently."

"Huh." Mina pinched her lips together, her eyes darting from side to side as she processed what Abby was saying. "What about the other messages?"

"Those were from Harvey. I think his first message was just from anger—he must have gone into the kitchen and picked up a piece of chalk and wrote what was on his mind: *Don't you know this place is a tomb?* That was right around when he'd first started working here. Then, when people freaked out, he kept up the messages, getting more and more elaborate over time. I'm not sure if he meant for people to think they were from Violet, at first, but when the rumors started spreading, he didn't stop them. He must have been hoping it would scare people away and the place would shut down."

"But it had the opposite effect, thanks to Sam." Mina tucked her hair behind her ears. "I'm sorry I ever suspected them."

"It's okay," Abby said, finding that she meant it. "You just wanted to keep me safe."

"I did." Mina took Abby's hand, intertwining their fingers together in a way that made Abby's heart flutter with warmth. "I have to say, this is officially the worst Valentine's Day ever. What do you say we have a do-over tomorrow?"

Abby grinned up at her. "I'd love that."

Returning her grin, Mina pulled Abby toward her for a kiss.

For the first time, Abby didn't worry about Chelsea or losing Mina or what the future would hold for them. She simply leaned into the kiss, savoring the gentle brushes of Mina's lips. They were warm and smooth and tasted faintly of coffee and pineapple ChapStick. Mina's fingers ran gentle patterns through Abby's hair, growing firmer and more desperate with every second. Abby leaned into her sturdy embrace, feeling vibrant and alive and more at ease than she had felt in a long time.

"Abigail Spector!"

Abby started at the sound of her full name. That sounded an awful lot like her mother's voice. She broke the kiss, turning to see who could be calling her. Sure enough, Rebecca Spector was storming up the front lawn.

"Mom?" Abby took in her oversized shirt and sweatpants— clothes her mother would rarely leave the house in unless something was *really* wrong—and her stomach knotted with dread. "What are you doing here?"

Chapter
Twenty-Three

"What are you doing starting house fires?" Rebecca shouted, loud enough to draw attention from half the nicely dressed guests scattered across the front yard.

"I didn't *start* it," Abby protested.

"I called," Rebecca snapped. "Four times. You didn't answer."

"My phone broke."

"Of course it did." Rebecca shook her head. "Always something with you. Can't keep anything alive—your plants, your phone—it seems like you're barely managing to keep yourself alive."

"Please tell me you didn't drive four hours just to scold me. You could have just called Lucas for that."

"I did! He didn't answer either."

Abby narrowed her eyes. The fire had started less than half an hour ago; there was no way her mom could get there in that amount of time. Which meant she wasn't checking up on Abby to make sure she was still alive. "What are you doing here, really?"

Her mother pursed her lips, checked her watch, and then chewed her lower lip, making it very clear she wasn't sure if she wanted to answer that question or not.

"Mom," Abby insisted. "What is it?"

"Well, it may be nothing now." She lowered her voice conspiratorially. "But I saw your post on social media—"

"You follow me?"

"Of course. Anyway, that post you made about Violet Love-less's boyfriend—I did some digging—"

Abby blinked. "Wait, were you trying to help me? With paranormal investigating?"

"—and I found out he's been working here the past three months."

Abby felt her lips twitch into a smile. Even though her mother wouldn't answer her question directly, the fact she had looked into anything was clearly her way of supporting her.

"That seemed pretty suspicious," Rebecca continued. "So, last night, I called to warn you, but I couldn't reach you. So I called Sam, who told me about the robbery—"

"It wasn't exactly a robbery," Abby protested, wondering what exactly Sam had told her mother. Abby doubted Sam had mentioned the attack, or her mother would be hysterical right now, threatening to sue the place.

"And Sam said they'd take care of it. But then Sam stopped answering their phone and my motherly instincts told me something was off—"

"Since when do you have motherly instincts?"

"I always have motherly instincts when it comes to you," Rebecca replied. "You just choose to ignore them, and I can't do anything about that. Anyway, here I am. At the perfect time, judging from the looks of things."

"Actually, the perfect time would have been about two hours ago, when Sam was locked in the pantry and we could have stopped Harvey from lighting the building on fire." Abby gestured to the house.

Rebecca scoffed, turning back to her watch. "Well, I should call your father and tell him you're okay. And then Sam's mother will want to know her child's okay, and that four of us will be coming for dinner."

"Six," Abby corrected. "Michelle and David are here too."

"Oh, are they?" Rebecca's face lit up. "They used the gift card I gave them."

Abby's suspicions were confirmed. "You used Sam's friends-and-family discount."

"It's a highly rated hotel," Rebecca said, turning her back to Abby. "I'll have to ask them how they liked the food."

"Before they were chased out by the fire?" Abby called after her.

Rebecca waved her off.

She turned back to Mina with a sigh. "You remember my mother?"

"Too well," Mina replied. Her fingers slid toward the binoculars around Abby's neck. "I take it Harvey stole these as well?"

Abby nodded. "He wanted to see Violet, but he didn't know where to look."

"I'm glad you got them back. They still work?"

"Let's see." Abby held her breath as she raised the lenses to her eyes and Mina faded to a wispy transparent gray. She brushed them across the smoky lawn, over spooky trees and echoes of past landscapes, until she saw the bright outline of a man in pajamas, with his arm draped around a dark-haired woman, standing barefoot on the front lawn, watching the fire.

"Charles!" Abby called. "Matilda!"

They turned to her. Charles gave a friendly wave while Matilda's lips twitched upward in the faintest hint of an approving smile.

Abby stepped toward them. "Thank you."

With a firm nod, they turned back toward the house.

"I'll take that as a yes?" Mina asked, bringing Abby back to the present. She let the binoculars fall, the world sharpening, growing bright with sirens and firelight.

"Yeah," Abby said, turning back toward Mina. "They still work."

"Great." Mina wrapped her arms around Abby's shoulders, pulling her close. "Now, where were we?"

Abby grinned as her lips returned to Mina's, the wails of sirens and crashes of burning wood faded to the back of Abby's mind until there was only the starlit sky and the warmth of Mina's embrace.

"I HAVE TO tell you, that was some nice detective work," Sam said between sips of nutty-smelling coffee from their oversized mug. They lounged casually in a lawn chair near their front door, their bathrobe open to reveal a faded *Rocky Horror Picture Show* T-shirt and sweatpants. "Minus the part where you left me in that box."

"In my defense, I didn't know you were in there. And I had bigger things to worry about. Like your coworker burning down the building." Abby took a seat in the chair beside them, dropping her luggage on the grass by her feet. A bird soared overhead, chirping as it landed in the bare maple tree to bask in the morning sunrise. It was hard to believe it was already Monday. Abby felt a surprising pang of sadness at having to leave this town, despite her near-death experiences.

Cupid's bark rose from the side of the house. He ran the distance of the fence, trying to get to the bird, or Sam—probably both.

Abby waved. "He seems to enjoy his new home."

Sam finished a large gulp of coffee before replying, "Yeah. Our yard's not as big as Willow's Edge, but he doesn't seem to mind. And it's only a short walk to the dog park."

Abby winced at the reminder that the bed and breakfast would be undergoing repairs and renovations for the foreseeable future. "Sorry we didn't stop Harvey sooner."

"It's not your fault." Sam waved a hand dismissively. "I'm sorry I hired him. Worst mistake I've ever made. But it'll be good to have some time off. Do some re-prioritizing. Focus on what really matters, you know?"

"Like friends?" Abby speculated. "Family?"

"I was thinking more along the lines of my personal social media. But I like your answer better." Grinning, Sam bent down and picked up a stick, which they tossed over the fence.

Cupid charged after it, his golden fur rippling in the wind.

Sam's face lit up with a sense of pride. They turned back to Abby with a shrug. "I'm glad you came. And not only because you saved my life. It's also just good to see you. You seem happier."

Abby leaned forward, running her nails along the pocket in her jeans. "Thanks?"

"It's just an observation," Sam said. "You're not the only one who can observe, you know. I like Mina. I think she's good for you."

Abby felt her cheeks warm as her lips tilted upward. "I think she is too."

But it wasn't just Mina that brought a lightness to her chest. It was the path she was on—spending time with Lucas, helping ghosts move on, even reuniting with Sam. She might not know what tomorrow would bring, but she trusted that it would be something *exciting*.

"Speak of the devil." Sam nodded toward the front door as it creaked open, and Mina stepped out, fully dressed, her gym bag hung over her shoulder.

Sam stood and stretched, clutching their mug at their side. "That's my cue to leave. I need more coffee anyway. I'll see you around."

"Take care," Abby called.

Sam waved without turning around, before heading inside. The screen door squeaked shut behind them.

Mina's combat boots crunched across the grass as she headed toward Abby, her lips wide with a grin. "I'm going to miss you."

"I already miss you." Abby stood and wrapped her hands around her waist, pulling her close.

"I'll call you tonight. And we can plan our next date." Mina kissed her forehead, making the ache in Abby's heart fade for a moment. "On second thought, maybe *I* should plan this one."

"You didn't like the spa and boat?" Abby asked, referring to the previous evening's activities using the last of her prizes from the chocolate festival.

Mina's eyes warmed with the hint of a smile as she straightened the scarf around Abby's neck. "Those were nice. But we could have done without staying in a hotel working alongside a creepy arsonist pretending to be a ghost."

"Fair enough."

Mina sighed, running her thumb along Abby's chin. "I've been thinking—"

Abby's heartbeat quickened. "Why does that sound like you're about to break up with me?"

Mina shook her head, the corners of her mouth twisting into a smile. "Not where I was going at all. I've been thinking that I really like you."

Abby grinned. "I could have told you that."

Mina moved her finger over Abby's lips. "*And* I want to be a really good partner to you. I haven't always been. A good partner, that is."

"I think you're doing great."

Mina's cheeks darkened with a faint blush. "Thanks. But I think I could be better. When we met, I'd been…kind of depressed. And then you came in with your optimism and enthusiasm and I just—I love being near you. You make me feel so *happy*."

"You're welcome," Abby said, returning her mouth to Mina's.

She felt Mina's lips twist into a grin under her own. When she stepped back, Mina's eyes sparkled. "So, my point was, I like you. I'm happy with you. But I should also be happy with myself."

Abby scrunched up her nose. "Are you sure you're not trying to break up with me?"

Mina laughed her sweet melodic laugh. "I'm sure. I'm just saying that I'm going to work on not putting so much pressure on you to make me happy. And I guess…that I might be messy at times."

"That's okay," Abby said. "I can be messy too."

The corners of Mina's eyes crinkled. Abby mentally traced every detail of her face—from the small scar over her lip to the faint freckles under her eyes to the exact shape of her warm brown eyes. She wished she could draw so she could capture it perfectly. "Maybe sometime, you'll let me see you messy."

Abby gulped, before nodding. If she wanted a relationship with Mina, she would have to be open with Mina, even if it was about Chelsea. "I still think of Chelsea. Sometimes."

"I think of my mom every day," Mina said softly.

"Right, but she's your mom," Abby said. "Chelsea is— *was*—my girlfriend."

"So?"

Abby took a deep breath. "So, sometimes I think about her when I'm with you. When we kiss and things. Sometimes."

Mina's head tilted in thoughtful concentration. "That makes sense. If you ever want to stop—"

"Then I'll tell you," Abby promised. "But right now, I'm not thinking of her. Just you."

Abby stood on her tiptoes to kiss Mina one final time, before letting Mina walk away.

Sighing, she returned to her car and slipped inside. It was already warm, the engine running, as Lucas bobbed his head along to the music in the passenger seat.

"You seem in a good mood." Abby shut the door behind her. In the rearview mirror, Mina's car moved down the driveway and out of sight.

"I may have told Dr. Greenwood about Matilda. She's

ecstatic. She's going to put her in her book."

"The one about Violet?"

"It's about the history of the bed and breakfast. Or it was. She was so excited about Matilda, I wouldn't be surprised if the whole book ends up being about her."

"I'm glad she's finally getting some attention."

"And, in exchange for this information, Dr. Greenwood may or may not have asked for my résumé."

"That's exciting!" Abby clapped Lucas's shoulder, excited for her friend, even though the thought of him taking a job in a different state made her stomach knot. "I'm proud of you."

"She didn't have an opening at Yale, but she knows the hiring manager of this full-time position open at Amherst. Said she'd put in a good word."

"That's great," Abby said, finding she genuinely meant it.

"You know, if I get this job, I'll be moving to Massachusetts."

"I know." Abby nudged Lucas's arm. "But we'll still be friends. And I'll come visit every weekend."

"Maybe not *every* weekend." Lucas adjusted his glasses. "But of course we'll still be best friends. I take it your date went well?"

Abby chewed her lip to stop her grin from spreading over her entire face. It didn't work. Lucas grinned back. "Mina's that good, huh?"

Abby teasingly punched his arm. "It was nice. Romantic. The perfect Valentine's Day."

"And here, I thought the perfect Valentine's Day was eating half-off chocolate." Lucas shrugged, but Abby could tell he was happy for her.

"Those are good too. Which reminds me." Abby reached into her bag and pulled out a giant heart-shaped box with a large red sticker on the front.

Lucas gasped. "Mina got you that?"

"Nope, this is for us. Fifty percent off. We had some time between the spa and our dinner reservations, so I stopped and picked it up. For the drive home."

Lucas snatched the box from her, tearing off the plastic. "You are the best friend ever."

"Don't you forget it." Grinning, Abby put the car in reverse and backed out of Sam's driveway. It was time to go home.

The End.

Abby and her friends will return in Book 3 of the Abby Spector Ghost Mystery series. Visit MorganSpellman.com to learn more.

Acknowledgements

Thank you to everyone who had a hand in the creation of this book, and to those of you who have supported me along my writing journey.

A special thank you goes out to my family—your love and support has made my writing career possible.

Kiran, I'm so glad I commented on your fanfic! You are the best wife I could have asked for. In addition to all of your support in daily life, I appreciate your feedback on my plot, characters, and finished drafts.

Thank you, April, for discussing story ideas with me. Grandpa, thank you for instilling in me a love of ghost stories at a young age. And, Grandma, thank you so much for spreading the word about the first book in this series!

A huge shout out to my line editor, Hannah McCall at Black Cat Editorial Services. I'm always impressed by the detailed feedback you provide. You made this story shine.

A special thank you to my beta readers, Zoe, Alaina, and

Tayla. Your thoughtful comments and suggestions have been invaluable in refining this story.

Holly Dunn, thank you for yet another gorgeous cover design! I'm always impressed with how well you capture the vibes of this series.

A big thank you to my dear friend, Kristi Langli, for being my biggest cheerleader. I don't know what I'd do without you!

I'm profoundly grateful for the wonderful community of readers who have continued to be a guiding force throughout my writing journey. To those of you who read, reviewed, and recommended Say I Boo—your support has not only made this second book possible but has infused it with a sense of shared excitement and anticipation. It's an absolute pleasure to continue sharing the tales of Abby and her friends with you. Thank you wholeheartedly for being such an integral part of this incredible journey!

About the Author

Morgan Spellman (they/them) writes quirky stories sprinkled with magic and wonder. They hold an MA in Creative Writing from Oxford Brookes University and a day-job teaching software at a technology company. They live in North Carolina with their wife, two attention-seeking cats, and an entire cabinet devoted to tea. When not crafting queer stories, Morgan can be found hiking through scenic trails, indulging in freshly baked cookies, or embarking on epic tabletop role-play game quests with friends.

They can be found online at **morganspellman.com**